ROSWELL 1947

Thomas Settimi

ROSWELL 1947

ISBN-13: 978-0-6158-2917-3
ISBN-10: 0-6158-2917-1

Sky Scientific Press
PO Box 184
Skyforest, California 92385

Cover photograph by Evert Wittteveen, Laguna Beach, California

Also by Thomas Settimi . . .

CONVERGENCE
Sky Scientific Press

Paperback (ISBN-13: 978-1-4196-6151-8)
2nd Edition 2012

eBook Edition June 2012

Author's Disclaimer

This is a work of fiction. The characters, organizations and other entities presented in this novel are either (1) fictional products of the author's imagination or (2) in those cases where like-named entities actually exist, they are used fictitiously and with no intent to portray conversations, actions or personal attributes as other than fictional.

Thomas Settimi
Lake Arrowhead, California
tsettimi@gmail.com

CHAPTER ONE

AMANDA WAS NO STRANGER to the very hallway and nurse's station that lay before her as she exited the elevator on the 4th floor of Skylar Hospital. Her father, Edward Marshall, had passed away here just two weeks earlier, after a long illness. She had made numerous visits in the preceding weeks and the twinge of sadness she felt in her heart returned momentarily to remind her of her loss. Despite the frequency of their recent past encounters, the nurse supervisor appeared not to recognize her.

"May I help you?"

"Yes, I'm here to see Dieter Hedrick." Amanda unconsciously pushed aside the strands of red hair that began to cascade down and in front of the left side of her face. The nurse supervisor stroked her workstation keyboard briefly and replied without looking up again.

"Room 411, end of the hall on the left."

Amanda Marshall was a freelance investigative reporter and this was to be her first meeting with the patient. Dieter Hedrick had read some of Amanda's prior work and was impressed with it, finding her writing style to be direct and hard-hitting. For this reason, he hoped that Amanda would be the journalist to document his story—to finally reveal the truth to the world concerning the events that he personally witnessed nearly sixty years earlier. In 1947, Colonel Dieter Hedrick, USAF now retired, was a young lieutenant serving in the Public Information Office at Roswell Army Air Field, New Mexico.

It was less than 24 hours since Amanda was called and asked to come. Time was of the essence as Dieter Hedrick's condition was terminal. Doctors gave him a week or two at most.

Amanda stopped at the open doorway and peered in. The room was small and dim, shades drawn. Dieter Hedrick was in the first hospital bed, closest to the door. The privacy curtain to the second bed was open, revealing no occupant. Colonel Hedrick's head and shoulders were elevated. His hair was full with not even a trace of a bald spot, but disheveled—a gray mop with a few black streaks. His eyes were closed, despite the fact that the television monitor mounted high on the wall opposite him was on. She stepped lightly to the side of the bed and leaned over.

"Colonel Hedrick?" The interrogative, delivered slightly above a whisper, was a question concerning his state of consciousness and not his identity. The Colonel opened his eyes and turned his head to see her face.

"Miss Marshall. Thank you for coming." He spoke slowly and softly, but his voice did not waver or break. "My sister told me not to expect you here before tomorrow and that you might not be able to come at all."

"It was no trouble. I've been in Millport for the last few weeks, just down the road, visiting my parents." Amanda Marshall's permanent home was in Arlington, Virginia. She didn't explain what had brought her to this locality for such an extended period of time.

The Colonel reached for the water glass on the tray in front him and Amanda observed that it was nearly empty.

"Let me help you," Amanda offered, then filled the glass two-thirds full from the yellow and white plastic water pitcher nearby. Colonel Hedrick drew a few sips from the drinking straw in the glass.

"Thank you." The Colonel pressed the mute button on the wired remote control that lay at his side, taking care to avoid the nurse call button on the keypad. The television that had been emitting barely audible sound when she first entered the room was now completely silent. He cleared his throat. "What do you know about the Roswell Incident?"

She thought for a moment, and then answered. "Not a great deal. I've read a few magazine articles over the years and seen occasional television reports. I confess that I don't remember many of the details. There was a crash site with the government claiming the debris was from a weather balloon or some such thing. How am I doing so far, Colonel?"

"Go on, Ms. Marshall."

"But then there are some people who believe it was an alien spacecraft and that bodies of the space travelers were recovered. That is about the extent of my recollection. From what I understand, it is still unresolved to this day."

"That is the general public perception. There are a few of us still living who know the whole truth of what happened sixty years ago. Are you still interested?"

Amanda Marshall retrieved a small digital recorder from her purse and placed it on the tray table in front of Dieter Hedrick. "That's why I'm here, Colonel."

CHAPTER TWO

MAC BRAZEL WAS EXHAUSTED and had turned in early on the evening of July 2, 1947, but he couldn't sleep. He was worried. The rainstorm that began after sundown was not expected to arrive for another twenty-four hours. Mac was the foreman of a large sheep ranch near the small town of Corona, New Mexico. His ranch hands had completed most of the work he had assigned on that Wednesday—repairing some fence lines and filling the gullies from the last storm that had made the dirt roads impassable in places—but he had also hoped to move a flock of animals to a grazing pasture that was less vulnerable to flash flooding before the arrival of the next storm. They had run out of daylight and the move would have to be delayed until Thursday.

Mac didn't become overly concerned until the wind picked up and the rain began to fall in sheets. He was angry with himself. He knew that storms during the monsoon season could not be reliably predicted as to either their timing or severity. His state of mind made sleep impossible, even after convincing himself that there was nothing he could do tonight to help the situation. When the storm cleared tomorrow, he would survey the damage and count his livestock losses. End of story.

But well before midnight the rain subsided as the storm seemed to move off to the west. The thunder was reduced to a low rumble and Mac Brazel finally drifted off to sleep. How long he was asleep, he doesn't know, but he was suddenly awakened by a loud roar coming from outside. Not exactly a thunder clap, but what else could it be? He was up and at the window in his bedroom in an instant. The sky was bright with lightning. So bright, in fact, that when he turned back to the room he could see his shadow on the headboard and the wall above it. It was curious, though, because no rain was falling. He watched for several minutes, until the brightness in the sky was thoroughly dissipated.

"Tomorrow is a big day," he thought to himself. "I've got to get some sleep."

"C'MON, TIM. We're burning daylight!" Little Timmy Proctor was the seven year old son of Mac Brazel's neighbor. He enjoyed nothing more than hanging around with Mac, especially on days like today when he could accompany the ranch foreman on horseback as he made his rounds.

"Where are we going today, Mr. Brazel?" The young man was a skilled rider for his age and quickly caught up with Mac.

"Got to check out the flock we left in the south pasture yesterday. It won't bother you much if we find some drowned sheep, will it?"

"No, sir."

The early morning sky was deep blue and cloudless. The air was cool and calm for now, but with a hint that it would not stay that way for very long this morning. Less than a mile before they reached the pasture—an overly generous term to describe the hillside plot of sparse, nondescript vegetation that lay ahead of them—Mac noticed some curious debris on the ground. From his height on horseback, it looked to Mac like pieces of a highly reflective metallic foil. A piece every few feet at first, but then more and more as they proceeded further south into the debris field.

"What do you 'spose that stuff is, Mr. Brazel?"

"Don't know. Why don't you hop down and grab me a few pieces?" Timmy Proctor did exactly that, and handed two of the larger pieces—about a foot square—up to Mac.

"Ever see anything like this before, Mr. Brazel?"

"Can't say as I have. Looks like some kind of airplane or weather balloon must have come down here." Mac compressed one of the pieces inside his fist and was surprised to see it return to its original shape—without a wrinkle—when Mac released it. "Well, I'll be dipped in shit . . . . You know, I think I heard this thing come down last night. Thought it was a thunderclap at first, but it must have been this crash."

In the next few minutes, Mac and Timmy gathered up some more pieces of the strange material. Mac was unable to cut it with his knife or tear it. Very strange stuff, indeed.

"When we get back to the ranch, I'll need to call out to Roswell Field and tell those folks what we found here, but first we still need to check on them sheep."

MAC AND TIMMY REMOUNTED the horses and set off on the last half-mile or so to where the flock was left the day before. When they arrived, Mac was surprised to find that apparently no sheep had been lost. Maybe the area had been spared the deluge that the ranch house itself had suffered the night before. Mac removed his hat and mopped the sweat off his forehead and back of his neck with a large red handkerchief, then surveyed the grazing area once more before calling out to Timmy, “C’mon Tim. These sheep will get along just fine until the boys get back here this afternoon. Let’s head home.”

CHAPTER THREE

COLONEL HEDRICK RAISED HIMSELF slightly in his hospital bed and took another sip from the water glass.

"So it was a weather balloon, then?" Amanda posed the half-question, half-statement. The Colonel smiled as he placed the glass back on the tray table.

"You mean, because of the reflective plastic film—the Mylar—that Mac Brazel and Timmy Proctor found that day?" Amanda nodded in the affirmative. "No, not a weather balloon, but certainly not something alien, either. When Mac got back to the ranch, he immediately phoned the base switchboard and the call was directed to Major Jesse Marcel, the base intelligence officer. He notified the base commander, and then he called me. I was told in no uncertain terms to get a team of military people out there—no civilians—and gather up every scrap of debris from the site. And that is exactly what we did. I even made Mac give up the pieces that he and Timmy had picked up."

"So, it wasn't a weather balloon but it wasn't anything alien, either. So why the concern of the base commander and all the controversy that followed?"

"You've got to consider the times we were living in—and the location. It had been less than two years since the first atomic test at Trinity Site in Alamogordo, conducted only ninety miles from the base. The Cold War with the Soviets was heating up and there were rumors that our nuclear secrets had been compromised. When President Truman met with Stalin in July 1945 and mentioned that we had a new super weapon, it is likely that the Soviet leader already knew about our successful first atomic test at Alamogordo just a few days earlier. Our scientists were anticipating the day that the Soviets would explode their first weapon and wanted above all to be able to detect and monitor Soviet testing. We didn't have today's seismic technology and spy satellites back in 1947, so Army Air Corps scientists developed a detection system using an array of balloons with microphones and radio transmitters. They called it Project Mogul. It was the fallen debris from one of those balloon arrays that Mac Brazel found on the morning of July 3rd."

Amanda tilted her head to one side. She wasn't buying the story. "Since when do balloons falling out of the sky cause an explosion like the one that Mr. Brazel heard the night before?"

"They don't," Colonel Hedrick grunted in approval of Amanda's perceptive question. "Nobody told Mac, but it was pretty obvious to any trained observer that the debris we picked up that day had come down several days—maybe even a week—earlier. The explosion that Mac heard was indeed the result of a crash, but not the one that resulted in the debris field that Mac discovered. What Mac heard was the crash of a single flying object some ten miles northwest of where the Project Mogul balloon array came down."

"So," Amanda asked, "how did the stories about extraterrestrials come about?"

"Actually, the accounts of a flying disc—what folks today would call a flying saucer, including those claiming that aliens were found inside—came out very early in local papers, but they were quickly squelched by the Army. Someone above my pay grade must have made the determination that a less exotic explanation was needed for public consumption; hence, the balloon debris story. But the alien accounts seemed to persist, and after a while the Army stopped commenting directly. I personally believe that the Government encouraged some of the more exotic theories. As years passed and the incident received world-wide attention, more theories began to emerge. Some of them were really far out. Amanda, you need to understand that our Government has been complicit in the advancement of all these screwball theories. Maybe not inventing them, but certainly encouraging virtually any cockamamie story that would lead the public away from the truth."

"Do you believe that obfuscation of the truth concerning Roswell is a continuing policy of the U.S. Government? Even after all these years?" As Dieter Hedrick considered Amanda's previous question, he noticed behind her one of the staff doctors and a nurse standing just inside the doorway to the room. The nurse was carrying an IV bag.

"Hi, Colonel Hedrick. I'm Doctor Simpson and wanted to look in on you." Without waiting for a reply, the Doctor walked forward to the bed and raised Dieter's left wrist to feel his pulse. "You seem a little dehydrated. Nurse Jenkins is going fix an IV to hydrate you a bit. Could your visitor excuse us for a few minutes? There's a waiting area next to the nurse's station." Dr. Simpson looked directly at Amanda. As she rose he added, "We'll come by and let you know when we're finished here."

In the waiting area, Amanda realized that she had left her voice recorder on the tray table in Dieter Hedrick's hospital room. She took out a notepad and began writing down her impressions of the Colonel and the history of the Roswell Incident that he had related to her. She appreciated the background details, but the story was just getting interesting and Amanda could hardly wait to hear what was coming next. Would the Colonel confirm the existence of dead extraterrestrials discovered at the Roswell crash site? Or would his testimony support the military's contention that nothing extraordinary happened there—that the little green men from outer space were simply part of the usual hype coming from the UFO wing of the conspiracy theory network.

After 25 minutes, Amanda finished her notes and began to check her watch, anxious to return to Colonel Hedrick's room. After 35 minutes, she could wait no longer and proceeded back toward Room 411. But finding the door was closed, she returned to the nurse's station.

"Excuse me, but Doctor Simpson and his nurse promised to find me after their session with Colonel Dieter Hedrick, but it's been a long time. Do you suppose it would be all right if I go back in now?"

"Doctor Simpson? We have no Doctor Simpson here. You must be mistaken."

Amanda insisted. "No, I distinctly heard the doctor's name. They were about to administer an IV."

"I don't think so." The nurse supervisor rose from her chair and walked around the counter in the direction of Colonel Hedrick's room. Amanda followed closely behind. "His chart clearly shows that he is in Hospice Care. No meds except for pain control . . ." She turned her head back towards Amanda. ". . . and no hydration except for what he can ingest by mouth."

When the nurse supervisor opened the door to Room 411, she found the patient in severe distress. Dieter Hedrick's head was slumped over to one side, nearly off the pillow. His eyes were closed and his mouth was open; he appeared to be unconscious. The IV bag was half empty and the line was still attached to his arm. There was no sign of the mysterious Dr. Simpson or the nurse that accompanied him.

The nurse supervisor quickly noted that the patient's status monitor was turned off and she immediately reset it. After a few seconds, the monitor confirmed her worst fear. Dieter Hedrick was near death with his blood pressure and respiration numbers well into the danger zone. His heart rate was slow and the beat irregular. The nurse supervisor tripped the Code Blue alarm and in less than one minute a team of medical personnel was in the room. Amanda Marshall stood by near the doorway with a horrified expression on her face. The medical team commenced at once to work on the patient.

After several minutes the team was able to temporarily restore sinus rhythm and a near normal heart rate. Colonel Hedrick opened his eyes and pulled off the oxygen mask so that he could speak.

"Amanda Marshall, please. . . . I need to speak with her now. . . . Please." His breathing was labored and he could hardly get out the words between breaths. Amanda immediately came forward and bent over to be close to the Colonel's face. "Wormstone," he whispered to her. "It's all about Wormstone."

Dieter Hedrick fell back into an unconscious state. Two minutes later his heart stopped and no attempt was made to revive him. The next day the nurse supervisor would be severely reprimanded for violating the DNR order that automatically came with Dieter Hedrick's status as a hospice patient. "I simply forgot," she later said. "When I found that the patient monitor had been turned off and no sign of that Doctor Simpson, well, I just went into automatic mode when I saw that the patient was coding. I'm sorry." She was cleared of all wrongdoing when the police investigation determined that the IV contained a dilute solution of morphine and potassium chloride and the hospital's video recording system confirmed the arrival and subsequent departure of the mysterious Dr. Simpson and his associate.

Amanda Marshall sat alone in the hospital room with Colonel Hedrick, his lifeless body and face covered with a bed sheet. There was no doubt in her mind that the Colonel's life was taken prematurely—if only by a few days—at the hands of a man who called himself Dr. Simpson and with the assistance of his "nurse" associate. Under what circumstances is the life of a terminally ill patient taken prematurely? In some cases pain medication is "liberally" dispensed to end the patient's suffering at the patient's request. But not in this case. Dieter Hedrick had a story to tell before he was to leave this world and he wanted Amanda to hear it. After considering all of the possibilities, Amanda was left with the only conclusion that made any sense. Dieter Hedrick was killed to keep him from telling his story—the story of the true facts surrounding the mystery of Roswell—to her as his designated confidant. Amanda also understood that by now, the perpetrators likely were aware that they had successfully accomplished their mission, for her voice recorder—with its compelling yet incomplete story—was nowhere to found in the hospital room, nor had it been seen by any of the hospital staff who came into the room in a vain attempt to save the Colonel's life.

Amanda didn't know exactly what had compelled her to remain in Dieter Hedrick's hospital room after the medical staff had left. She felt bad for the Colonel. Despite his terminal condition, she considered his death to be unquestionably tragic. Maybe it was in some strange way her sense of the disappointment that he no doubt would have felt about being prevented from telling his story. Or maybe she was simply feeling her own loss at no longer having a good story—or at least not an easy one—to tell.

"YOU REALLY SHOULDN'T be in here, you know." The man in the suit and tie spoke sternly and Amanda was startled by his tone.

"I'm sorry . . . ?"

"This room—it's a possible crime scene, and if we determine that a murder took place here, we don't want any evidence to be compromised."

"I'm sorry. Are you with the police?"

"Schuyler County Sheriff's Office. I'm Investigator Matthew Gallo. And you are . . . ?"

Amanda rose from her chair. "Amanda Marshall. I was interviewing the Colonel. And why did you call this a *possible* crime scene? Isn't it obvious?"

"Not at all. I understand that Colonel Hedrick was terminal. Maybe it was just his time. It will take an autopsy to be sure."

"But that Doctor Simpson—the desk nurse said there's no such physician on the staff here."

"That's what I want to ask you about: why do you think someone would want to kill the Colonel, knowing he was terminal?"

"I don't mean to sound self-absorbed, but I was interviewing Colonel Hedrick for a very important story."

"What kind of story?"

"Colonel Hedrick was stationed in Roswell, New Mexico in 1947. You've heard of the Roswell UFO incident?"

"Who hasn't?" Amanda detected a snicker in the investigator's reply. "You're suggesting that the story he had to tell was so shocking, so—" Investigator Gallo paused, raising both hands in mock emphasis that words were simply inadequate to describe the magnitude of this bombshell story. "—so explosive indeed—that he had to be silenced, lest the truth be revealed." Amanda did not appreciate the sarcasm.

"Unfortunately, I didn't hear the whole story, but it is pretty clear to me that the suspects—no, the murderers—wanted to keep the Colonel from talking. They even took my voice recorder."

Matthew Gallo paused to weigh Amanda's words before responding. "OK. Sorry for being so skeptical; just my nature, I guess. We'll know for sure in a couple of days." The investigator removed a pen and pad from his inside coat pocket. "Can you describe the suspects?"

"What can I tell you? He looked like a doctor—maybe forty-five, medium height and build. She was mid-thirties, about my height but heavier, with short blonde hair—bleached."

"Anything unusual, Ms. Marshall, that you can recall about the couple or what you saw or heard today?"

"Sorry, nothing else comes to mind."

ON THE DRIVE BACK TO MILLPORT, Amanda wrestled with a decision she had to make. The logical and probably smartest thing she could do would be to simply walk away from the notion of following up another new angle in the often told and controversial history of Roswell. While only vaguely familiar with some of the theories surrounding the events of 1947, she knew at least that no single theory had as yet been proven beyond a reasonable doubt. If not a single one of the hundreds of Roswell researchers was able to uncover the truth in the past sixty years, what chance did she have? Not much of one, she thought; especially after having lost the eyewitness-to-history deathbed testimony of Colonel Dieter Hedrick.

Amanda understood the magnitude of the task before her should she determine to proceed with this project. And without some competent help, the odds were that she would fail. It was with great reluctance that she decided to seek that help.

CHAPTER FOUR

IT'S A FOUR-HOUR DRIVE from Millport, New York, to Gettysburg, Pennsylvania. Along the way, Amanda Marshall had nearly turned back twice—once as she crossed Interstate 80 and again just outside of Harrisburg. She was ambivalent. Roger Atwood, Professor of History at Gettysburg College and known for his competent and tenacious research, was her obvious choice as the most qualified individual she knew to help unravel the mystery of the Roswell Incident. But it was history—their history together—that was the problem. She and Roger were together as a couple for only a few months and it ended badly more than one year ago.

Amanda made no attempt to contact Roger Atwood before she arrived on the campus, but a call to the History Department Office told her what she needed to know. Professor Atwood would be lecturing in his class entitled "Civil War Era Studies" in the same building and room in which she first sat under his teaching three years earlier. She parked near the chapel and proceeded to the Weidensall Hall Classroom Building on Washington Street. Amanda waited outside the door to Room 302. She could hear Roger as he was wrapping up his lecture.

His command of the subject and the class reminded her of why she had been attracted to him in the first place. She was sorry it hadn't worked out between them and felt a flutter inside as the class bell rang and his students spilled out of the classroom and into the hallway. Would he think she was there in an attempt to reestablish their failed relationship? She hoped not. She would have to make that clear right from the beginning.

He was marking the day's stopping point in his lecture notes and didn't look up until she spoke.

"Hello, Roger." He was stunned. He stepped around the lectern and stood before her momentarily before extending his arms and embracing her.

"It's so good to see you. You look great!"

"Roger, I'm here because I need your help—with a new project. Can we go somewhere where we can talk and get some lunch? I've been on the road all morning and I'm starved."

AMANDA MARSHALL and Professor Atwood exited the west side of the building and passed the Musselman Library in the direction toward the College Union Building. It was warm for early December and Amanda removed her raincoat. Roger walked beside her, hands in the pockets of his trousers and looking down at the foot path.

"I didn't expect to see you again—after the last time we spoke together. How long has it been?" Roger didn't need to ask the question. He knew exactly how long it had been since their very last time together in Washington DC.

"It's been at least a year, I think."

"Yeah, I guess it's been that long. And I'm really sorry about your dad."

"Thanks. You know you could have called if you wanted to talk. I mean, just because we were no longer together, it didn't mean that I never wanted to speak with you again."

"I've been really busy. I had a full class schedule last spring and taught both summer sessions. Before I knew it, the fall semester had started." It wasn't exactly true. He hadn't been that busy. But he was hurt over their breakup and in the last six months had become depressed over it.

In the College Union Building, Amanda seated herself at a table for two in one corner of the Bullet Hole Restaurant while Roger ordered and waited for a turkey sandwich for Amanda and a bowl of clam chowder for himself.

"So tell me. . . ." Roger moved the vacant chair around to be next to Amanda and continued, "What's this new project all about?"

"Roswell, New Mexico—1947," she answered.

Roger snickered, "You're kidding."

"No, not at all."

"Why on earth would you want to get involved with that old, tired story? It's been examined six ways from Sunday."

Amanda was visibly irritated. "Why would you try to dismiss the project with such an old and tired expression like 'six ways from Sunday' before you even heard what I had to say about it?"

"OK." Roger paused and looked down briefly. "You're right, Amanda. I'm sorry. Tell me the whole story. What is it all about?"

Instead of responding immediately, she gave Roger a brief penetrating squint as if she considered making no response at all, but then she began. "Last week I was interviewing a retired Air Force officer who was an eye witness to the events at Roswell in

1947. He was giving what was tantamount to deathbed testimony."

"And?"

"And he was murdered during a break in the interview when I was asked to leave his hospital room. It was horrible. There is no doubt in my mind that Dieter Hedrick was killed to keep him from telling his story."

"Murdered? Who murdered him?"

"A couple pretending to be a doctor and nurse. Maybe they were a real doctor and nurse. I don't know. They were never apprehended."

"So you're telling me that you really never heard his version of what transpired at Roswell? You still don't know if there was a cover up—if Roswell was all about weather balloons or little green men. Is that right?"

"No, that's not right. That there was a cover up is self-evident from the fact that Colonel Hedrick believed that his interpretation of the Roswell events—the version of the truth from his perspective—had never been told before. What other purpose would he have in calling me to his deathbed? And why are you so negative about all this, Roger? Frankly, I'm a bit surprised."

"I guess I don't understand where you can go with this story. You lost your primary source of information before you even started."

"Not completely. Before he died, the Colonel told me to check out something called 'Wormstone'. Have you ever heard of it?"

"Yes. I've heard that name. The Wormstone Group was an engineering services contractor. They were into weapons evaluation—missiles, mainly, for both the Navy and Air Force. This was years ago. I believe they had an office near DC, just outside the Beltway."

"Do you know if they had any connection to Roswell?"

"No, but I can look into it for you, if you'd like."

"I was hoping that we could look into it together."

Roger became agitated. "What do you want from me, Amanda?"

"I just thought that you might be interested in pursuing this investigation with me—to find out what really happened in Roswell, New Mexico, in 1947."

"You mean like our last successful investigation?"

Amanda slowly shook her head. She hated Roger's sarcastic tone. His pervasive negative view of things was one of the reasons she had ended their relationship. "It wasn't our fault, Roger. The government asked us—rather warned us—to keep the story of Nathaniel Booth out of the press. We had no choice." She spoke in a subdued tone, looking about for anyone within earshot.

Clearly, the return of the U.S. Navy pilot from Vietnam after thirty-five years missing in action had stirred tremendous national and international interest. But disclosure of the breathtaking details of the event—suppressed by the U.S. Government—would have been earth-shattering by comparison. The very existence of the extraordinary cosmic phenomenon that thrust the airman back—and later forward—in time would have been a news story of immense significance. Keeping a lid on the story was an anathema to everything that Amanda had strived for in her career. But the Government visitor—allegedly from the NSA—on that day in July more than two years ago was persistent. Their silence was expected as a matter of national security with the not-so-subtle threat of a criminal investigation and prosecution should they ignore the warning.

"I'm sorry we let the Government intimidate us into silence," Roger lamented.

"The moratorium is only temporary. Remember, they said it would be lifted eventually. Once they approve the release of my article, we'll get full credit for our work."

"And you believe that?"

Amanda rose from her chair. "Just forget it, Roger. I'm sorry I came here today." She sprinted toward the restaurant exit. Amanda was outside the College Union Building before Roger caught up with her.

"Amanda, wait," he called out. She turned to face him. "I'm sorry. I've been a little moody lately, I know. I didn't mean to take it out on you. Count me in, if you'll still have me. Where do you want to start? And when?"

"Obviously, we'll need to get to New Mexico, sooner or later. I'd like to start as soon as you can. Are you going to be available during your Christmas break?"

"As a matter of fact, I will be in Santa Fe for ten days—you know, my regular winter escape—but I can postpone it."

"Don't do that yet. Maybe just shorten it by a few days. I can join you for a side trip to Roswell. It can't be that far from Santa Fe. While you're sunning yourself, I'll go home and see what I can find out about the Wormstone Group in Washington."

Roger looked down at his watch. "You know, I wish we could spend some more time together this afternoon, but I have another class in ten minutes."

"That's OK. I need to get home anyway."

He gave her a peck on the cheek and said, "I'll call to get your itinerary. I can pick you up at the airport in Santa Fe."

"Good. See you soon." They parted company, but when only a few steps apart, Amanda stopped and called out, "Roger—" He walked back to where she was standing.

"What is it, Amanda?"

"I'm sorry, Roger, I should have mentioned it when we were discussing this earlier, but you should know that I told my sister all about Nathaniel Booth and the research we did for his mother. I left out no details."

"You mean, Suzanne? You shouldn't have; doesn't she work for the State Department?"

"She used to, but she lost her job after the last election, when the new Administration took over."

"Well, I hope she can keep a secret!"

"Me, too. She seemed really interested in Volume Three of that history book from the pawnshop. She wanted to know who else knew about our research project for Rose Booth."

CHAPTER FIVE

SHE HAD BEEN AWAY from her home in Crystal City for a few weeks, so after parking and dropping her luggage inside the door of her 6th floor loft condominium, Amanda Marshall headed for the Safeway Grocery on the basement level to replenish her cupboard and refrigerator.

She filled the grocery cart and at the check stand decided to pay the extra fee to have everything delivered upstairs to her condo. Finally, with the groceries put away and the first of several loads of clothes agitating their way to a state of cleanliness, Amanda poured a drink and seated herself in front of her Mac notebook computer. After startup, she checked her email account—nothing noteworthy since the day before— then opened the Safari browser, tabbed over to the Google search box and typed the word "Wormstone." There were over twenty thousand references to the word cited by Google.

"Wormstone is a pretty common name," Amanda thought to herself after perusing the list of multiple references to 'Wormstone' on page one and two of the search engine listing. Plenty of authors, doctors and professors and even a hamlet in England with the same name. On page three, she found it: "Wormstone Engineering Services, Inc." Clicking on the link brought her to a directory pages listing under the category "Engineering Services." The listing showed an address on Maple Street in Vienna, Virginia, but no phone number or web address. Not very informative, she thought.

Next, she tried searching on "Wormstone Engineering" but the only result returned was the same single engineering services reference found previously—a dead end. Amanda gave up after a few more unproductive searches.

VIENNA, VIRGINIA, IS A SLEEPY home town for thousands of government employees and contractors working in and around Washington DC. The town lies 15 miles west of the Capitol and about the same distance from Amanda Marshall's home in Crystal City.

She rounded the block twice, failing at first to notice what should have been the unmistakably large number "2200" on the side of the Fidelity Commerce Bank building on Maple Street. There was no attendant at the gate arm entrance to the parking garage. Amanda pushed the button and snatched the ticket that was served up toward her open driver's window, silencing that annoying buzzer. She found an open parking space on the second level and walked to the office building entrance. The building directory indicated that this level was occupied by a dental implant center; the bank was on the ground level. Several businesses were listed for the third and fourth floors, but there was no listing for Wormstone

Engineering. She entered the elevator, determined to head down a level and ask for help, but when she noticed there was a button for the fifth floor, apparently omitted from the building directory, she pushed it.

"MAY I HELP YOU?" The receptionist at the desk in the no-name lobby posed the question as if she were addressing another hopelessly lost dental patient.

"Is this Wormstone Engineering?"

"Yes, but unless you have an appoint—"

"I'm sorry," Amanda interrupted. "I would have called first, but I could find no phone listing." She presented her business card. "My name is Amanda Marshall, and I'm doing research for an article on engineering services contractors around the Beltway. I was hoping a manager might be available for a short interview."

The receptionist studied Amanda's face for several seconds, looking for any hint of insincerity, as she considered the request. Finally, she responded. "Due to the nature of our work here, we usually don't grant interviews to the press, but . . . ." The receptionist rose from her desk. "Why don't you wait in our conference room and I'll see if there is someone who can see you?" Amanda was led into an adjoining room. The receptionist left her there and closed the door.

The large rectangular wooden table and eight upholstered chairs were sized appropriately for the spacious conference room. A telephone and speaker were at the center of the table. There were no other pieces in the room—not even a waste basket—and only the single doorway and no windows to the outside. But a few framed photos and documents were mounted on one of the walls parallel to the long side of the table. Amanda walked over for a closer look.

The first framed item was an article from *Beltway Magazine* from August 2004 with the title "Local Engineering Firm Celebrates 60 Years in Business." Clearly, a puff piece from a local techno-business rag, hoping—or more likely, payback—for an ad contract. The second item was a photograph of a man in his late fifties or early sixties with thick black hair, streaked with gray, and combed straight back. The man was dressed in a gray suit and stood behind a lectern. A caption on the photo read, "Dr. Leonid Tushenkov Rejoins Wormstone Group as Technical Director after Several Years in Government Service."

Amanda's attention was next drawn to a black-and-white glossy photo depicting four men posing with shovels, standing in a vacant lot surrounded by scrub vegetation. The photograph contained some white specks that were clearly not a part of the scene indicating that this was a reprint of the original photo. The caption read, "Company Founder, Dr. Thomas Stark (left), formerly of Bell Laboratories, at Ground Breaking Ceremony for Wormstone Engineering Roswell Facility, April 10, 1944." Amanda remarked to herself that she had learned more about Wormstone Engineering in the last five minutes than the half-hour of internet research from the night before.

"Excuse me, Ms. Marshall?" It was the receptionist.

"I'm sorry. I was reading about your company. Very interesting."

“Good news. I spoke with Doctor Tushenkov, our new Technical Director, and he has agreed to meet with you for an hour if you can come back tomorrow at 10 AM.” She continued, “You should know that one month ago, before Doctor Tushenkov came aboard, you probably would have been escorted out of the building by security. The new TD has promised that our company will be more open to the press and public in the future.”

“I really appreciate your help.” Amanda was sincere. “I’ll be back in the morning.”

CHAPTER SIX

"THANKS FOR AGREEING to meet with me, Doctor Tushenkov." Amanda was seated next to the Technical Director in the same conference room in which she had waited the day before.

"Not a problem." The accent was minimal, but clearly of Russian origin, consistent with the Doctor's name. "You may not know, but our paths nearly crossed not too long ago. We have a mutual acquaintance."

"And who would that be?" Amanda's interest was now piqued.

"The Navy flyer, Nathaniel Booth. The agency I worked for before coming here was very much interested in his. . . " Long pause. ". . . his experience." Amanda was immediately unsettled. This was unexpected. How should she respond? She was unsure.

"You probably know, then, that Nathaniel Booth's experience is a subject that I have been cautioned not to discuss."

Tushenkov laughed. "Yes, I am aware. It was my former agency that issued the gag order."

"Thank you for that," replied Amanda sarcastically.

He gestured with a dismissive wave of his right hand. "That is all history. What can I do for you today, Ms. Marshall?"

"Maybe you could start by you telling me a little about your company. I couldn't seem to find much in the public domain. Most of what I have learned came from those documents on the wall behind us—that I saw yesterday." Amanda glanced up at the wall behind Tushenkov.

"Most of our work has been under NASA and DoD contracts, and most of it classified."

"Any projects that I might recognize?"

"Probably not. But we recently completed some work on a hypersonic propulsion system design for NASA. That project was unclassified. What specifically are you interested in?"

"Economic concerns are always of interest to my readers. I'm trying to determine if engineering firms in the area—such as yours—are preparing for the possibility of deep cuts in defense spending when Congress reconvenes in January." Amanda thought it was a reasonably good question, considering that it had nothing to do with her real purpose in coming to visit Wormstone Engineering.

"And tell me, Ms. Marshall, if you would: which other firms in the area have you interviewed concerning this scintillating topic?" She had no answer for Tushenkov. "What is it that you really want to know? Why did you come here yesterday—and today?"

She paused before replying, considering for a moment whether to continue her cover story, or instead admit that her stated premise for the visit was not exactly true. "OK, if you insist, I'll tell you what is on my mind today. The questions are quite simple. One, what is the connection between Wormstone Engineering and the Roswell UFO incident?"

"I don't know that there was any connection. Yes, Wormstone was first established with a facility in Roswell, but that was well before the alleged UFO incident. The company had several contracts with the Army Air Corps—later the Air Force—in New Mexico during and after the Second World War. I believe that our Roswell facility was permanently closed sometime before 1970, after the base closure. Any company records from that period would have been destroyed long ago. I can't help you with that one. What else?"

"What do you know about the death of Colonel Dieter Hedrick?"

"I heard of it only yesterday for the first time; somewhat troubling in view of the reported circumstances of his passing. I understand that he'd become delusional in the last weeks of his life."

"You probably are already aware that I was present when he died—excuse me—I should say, when he was murdered. I can assure you that his mind was quite clear."

"Then you were close to the Colonel?"

"No. I'd never met or spoke with him before the day he was killed. I was there to hear his version of the Roswell Incident, but he died before getting to the meat of his story. Before he passed, he urged me to check out your company. Do you know why he would ask me to look into Wormstone Engineering?"

"I believe I have already answered that question to the best of my ability." The Technical Director rose from his chair, signifying that he was bringing the interview to a close. Amanda extended her right hand as she rose.

"I wish I could say that you have been helpful, Doctor, but then I'd be lying. But thank you, anyway." Tushenkov shook her hand limply and smiled, his head cocked to one side. "One final question. . ." She pointed at the photo of Tushenkov on the wall behind the lectern. "The caption states that you recently rejoined Wormstone after a stint with the Government. When were you with the company previously?"

"Wormstone was kind enough to offer me a position when I first emigrated from the Soviet Union. That was in 1976. I remained with the company for five years." She acknowledged the answer with a nod and then turned toward the doorway to the office lobby.

"Ms. Marshall," Tushenkov called out to get her attention. She looked back at the Technical Director.

"Yes, Doctor?"

"I don't believe that the death of Colonel Hedrick and the historical events surrounding Roswell are in any way related, but sometimes the best decision we can make is to leave some questions unanswered." Amanda turned away, offering no response to Tushenkov's comment.

CHAPTER SEVEN

AMANDA STOPPED AT A BOOKSTORE near her home on Wednesday before leaving Washington DC. There were several titles in the 'conspiracies' section dealing with the Roswell Incident. She selected three to take on her flight, basing her selections primarily on the credentials of the authors.

The American Airlines flight from Dulles International early on a Thursday morning connected with another AA flight from Dallas-Fort Worth, arriving at Santa Fe Municipal Airport before noon. As previously arranged, Roger Atwood was waiting in his rental car outside the baggage claim area.

"Good flight?" he asked, helping her stow her bag in the trunk.

"Uneventful."

"Are you hungry? Or should we get on the road?" From Roger's tone, he seemed to be angling for the latter.

"Let's go; if you promise we can stop on the way."

"Well . . . ."

"What's up? What are you thinking?"

"Maybe we should find something in town here. It's three hours to Roswell and from the map, well—"

"—not much between here and there? Is that what you're trying to say?"

"Exactly. But let's not take too long. A good portion of the drive will be at high elevation. I don't want to get caught in a snow storm if the weather turns ugly. I'd like to get to the hotel before dark."

"OK, how about a drive-thru burger place?"

Roger exited the airport and pulled into the drive-thru at the McDonald's Restaurant on Airport Road and ordered for Amanda.

"You're not hungry, Roger?"

"Not very. I had a late breakfast. It will hold me until dinner." Roger passed the bag of burger and fries to Amanda and placed her drink in one of the cup holders next to her seat. He exited the drive-thru lane and continued east on Airport Road, then picked up Highway 285 South, toward Roswell.

"After you called the other evening, I checked for myself— you were right. There isn't much info out there about Wormstone Engineering."

"What, Roger? You didn't believe me?"

"That's not the point. It just seemed especially odd to me that a company currently in business, with a corporate headquarters and major government contracts—classified or not—doesn't even have so much as a corporate website." Amanda uttered a barely audible acknowledgement as she sipped the last of her cola. "But I called a friend yesterday—a retired Navy civilian—a former GS-many program manager for Naval Sea Systems Command in DC. He retired from the Navy about ten years ago. He told me that at one time early in his career he'd managed several contracts with the Wormstone Group. All pretty small ones—none over a hundred thousand dollars. The contracts were for reliability and maintainability analysis of Navy search radars and surface-to-air missile systems."

Amanda asked, "Is there any possible connection here—to Roswell?"

"I don't think so—the contract work was assigned to their Virginia office—but when I asked if he knew your Doctor Tushenkov, he told me he had met him once at a company cocktail party years ago—said that Tushenkov was hired by Wormstone for his work in stealth technology in the former Soviet Union."

"Stealth? That's what makes airplanes invisible to radar, right?"

"Exactly right! What's interesting is that it was the Soviets that are responsible for U.S. leadership in the field. There was a Soviet physicist named—"

Amanda interrupted him. "Why do I have the feeling that I am about to get another history lesson?"

"This is really interesting, Amanda. This Soviet physicist—his name was Petr Ufimtsev—publishes a paper on electromagnetic wave reflection and radar detection in the early sixties. The Soviets allowed it to be released because it supposedly had only academic value—no military application. But some ten years later, a Lockheed engineer is studying a U.S. Air Force translation of Ufimtsev's work. He does a preliminary engineering feasibility study and takes it to the head of his Lockheed research group. Lockheed wins a big development contract, followed by an even bigger production contract. All this work was done in complete secrecy. Experts believe that it was Ufimtsev's paper and the secrecy surrounding the subsequent development that made and has kept the U.S. the world leader in stealth technology."

"That was a very interesting tidbit of history, Roger. Thank you so much for sharing."

He smiled. "I can't help but sense a tone of insincerity in your words of appreciation, Amanda."

"Not intentional, I assure you. But on a more serious note, we have yet to establish a connection between the Roswell incident and Wormstone. Tushenkov is involved. Somehow, I believe he is a key figure in all of it."

As Roger passed through Encino, New Mexico, and continued on the road to Roswell, Amanda Marshall drifted off to sleep.

ROGER BARELY PAID ATTENTION to the white pickup truck pulling on to Route 285 behind them from a side street in the little town of Vaughn. But after a few miles, the truck seemed to be pacing them, maintaining a steady hundred-foot distance behind. Coming down from the 6,000 foot level in Vaughn to the lower elevation beyond, the light snow accumulation at the shoulder of the road at the higher elevation had now completely disappeared. Roger slowed to 45 mph, thinking that the truck might pass, but instead it slowed down to maintain the same hundred-foot separation. He then sped up—to 85—but the truck in Roger's rear view mirror did likewise, following close behind.

Between the towns of Vaughn and Mesa, while Roger and Amanda were still 70 miles north of Roswell, the white pickup moved to the fast lane and then slowly pulled forward, next to Roger and maintained the position. Roger could see the driver clearly—a white man, probably in his forties, wearing dark glasses and a baseball cap, with maybe a three-day growth of beard. The driver pretended to be fixated on the road ahead, acting as if he were oblivious to Roger's vehicle only a few feet away on his immediate right. By now, Amanda had awakened from her catnap.

"What is that idiot trying to do?" she exclaimed.

"I have no idea."

"Do you think you pissed him off somehow?"

"I don't know. I don't believe so."

Up ahead, Roger saw an immediate problem. A utility truck in the left lane, signaling for a turn at an upcoming intersection had slowed way down, but the white pickup showed no sign of letting up.

"You'd better back off, Roger, and let this guy get around you." But it was too late. Before Roger had a chance to respond, the white pickup sped up and began crowding into Roger's lane to pass between Roger and the utility truck. The right rear fender of the white pickup clipped Roger's front fender and then sped ahead. Roger was able to maintain control and pulled off on the right hand shoulder. The driver of the utility truck left his vehicle in the turn area between the lanes of the divided highway and ran over to Roger's car.

"Are you folks all right? I saw that guy coming up fast behind me. I thought for sure he'd slow down."

"We're OK," Roger replied. He was out of the car surveying the damage to his fender.

"It could have been a lot worse. Did you get his license plate?"

"No plates on that truck," Roger answered.

"I think you can still drive it—don't see any damage to your wheel or tire."

"That's something, I guess."

IT WAS QUIET IN THE CAR for the next ten miles. Finally, Amanda broke the silence. "Are you upset, Roger?"

"Just thinking."

"Were we targeted, or was that guy just some random crazy-ass driver?"

"My guess is that someone is trying to send us a message."

"You really think so?"

"The accident by itself could be random, but add the murder of your Colonel Hedrick—it could be that someone just doesn't want us going to Roswell. We can give this up if you want. I can turn around and we can spend the weekend together in Santa Fe."

"I don't think that would be a good idea. Besides, it's only a few more miles to Roswell."

"OK, it's your call. But don't you think we should cancel one of the rooms at the hotel? Just in case there is a real threat out there?"

"I know you are only concerned about my safety, Roger, but sharing a room would be an especially bad idea." Roger had no response.

CHAPTER EIGHT

AFTER DINNER, and before retiring to their separate rooms, Roger and Amanda agreed to meet for breakfast at eight AM. But it was nearly 8:30 before Amanda joined Roger in the hotel coffee shop. Roger was finishing his second cup of coffee.

"Sorry I'm late, Roger."

"No problem. I hope you slept well."

"Not very. I guess our little accident did upset me some." The waitress poured coffee for Amanda and asked if they were ready to order. "Just an English muffin for me." Roger ordered scrambled eggs and bacon. "What's the plan for the day?"

"I called the rental car agency. They want me to file a police report for the hit and run. And we're going to get another vehicle—something more substantial than that little sedan. There's a rental office not far from here. Then we start snooping around."

AFTER BREAKFAST, ROGER AND AMANDA drove to the Enterprise Agency on South Main Street. The rental associate surveyed the damage to the fender of their car, and then carefully examined the rental contract that Roger had signed in Santa Fe.

"Fortunately, Doctor Atwood, you signed for the optional collision coverage on this vehicle, so you won't be responsible for the damage. The crew is still cleaning up the replacement you requested. It should only be a few more minutes."

An hour later, Roger maneuvered the dark green Jeep Wrangler—the larger four-door Unlimited version—out of the agency lot and headed north on South Main Street. The public library, only a mile away on Pennsylvania Avenue, was easy to find thanks to the directions provided by the Enterprise rep.

"DO YOU WANT TO CHECK the electronic card catalog, or see if they have a newspaper archive?"

"I'll ask about the archives," replied Roger. "Why don't you see what you can find in the card catalog?"

But after fifteen minutes, Amanda joined Roger in the library reference room.

"I couldn't find a thing," she said. "Not a single entry in the card catalog for 'Wormstone'. Are you having any luck?"

"Nothing so far. The reference librarian told me they had a fire in the mid sixties and lost most of their early newspapers and magazines. The remaining old material is pretty hard to read. They probably dumped all the hard copies of the publications after putting them on microfiche years ago, so they had to scan the microfiche when they computerized everything. Resolution is pretty bad. I'm checking out *The Roswell Daily Record*. It was the most popular local paper at the time, but the index showed there was a competing publication, *The Roswell Morning Dispatch*. Why don't you see what you can find?"

Amanda sat down at the workstation next to Roger and the two spent the next hour and a half examining the incomplete archives of the two Roswell newspapers. Despite the missing volumes, they nonetheless found plenty of articles concerning the original 1947 incident and the investigations that followed. Readers apparently couldn't get enough of the accounts of government agencies and independent researchers who descended on the town over the years with a fierce determination to uncover the real story behind the UFO incident. A single notion seemed to run through most of the editorials. That is, that a government conspiracy was to blame for the lack of full disclosure and was responsible for suppression of the truth.

But the poor quality of the images made their work especially tedious. And while they found some interesting material—like the reporter interviews of Mac Brazel and Jesse Marcel conducted before Brazel died in 1963—they couldn't find a single reference to Wormstone Engineering.

Roger was perplexed. "If what Tushenkov told you was true, that Wormstone had a facility in town for maybe twenty-five years during and after the war, we should have been able to find some reference to it somewhere in these newspaper files." He continued, "If I were a suspicious person, I might think that the fire was intentionally set so that there could be an acceptable explanation for why the records are incomplete."

"Are we done here?" Amanda asked. "I'm getting hungry, and I've got a terrible headache trying to read the fuzzy print in those newspaper articles."

"We're pretty close to our next stop. Let's leave the car here and walk."

LUNCH WAS A SANDWICH AND SODA at Schlotzsky's Deli. They spoke little. Amanda took special note of the procession of what appeared to be tourists—mainly families with children—who came and left. As they left the deli, Amanda stopped and turned to face Roger. "Don't you think it's a little odd?"

"What's odd?"

"This town. Look around. Practically everything we've seen here since we arrived is aliens and UFOs. The whole town revolves around an incident that may or may not have taken place here nearly sixty years ago. Amazing."

Roger made a supporting observation. "Back at the hotel, I saw a brochure promoting their Annual UFO Convention. It attracts thousands of visitors each year. A lot of it is simply for fun—you know, with alien costumes and such—but apparently they also have some well-known speakers with lectures on serious topics, like astronomy and space travel. But even the wacky stuff is harmless, and you can't really fault the town for trying to capitalize on its history."

"So, where to next, Roger?"

"Actually, we are almost there." He paused. "I give you . . ." as he pointed to the marquee on what appeared to be a converted circa-1950 movie theater up ahead, " . . . the International UFO Museum and Research Center."

"You're kidding!"

Just inside the entrance, they were greeted by a large plastic alien holding a welcome sign. But this whimsical beginning of their museum tour soon gave way to a more serious and purposeful presentation of both known facts and unlikely speculations concerning the 1947 Roswell Incident. As they proceeded along the self-guided tour, they saw hundreds of photos and articles, describing in detail the crash site, witness accounts and official response of the Army and other agencies. One section was devoted to facts and speculation surrounding the possible cover-up of events by the U.S. Government. Another described the work of researchers, including excavations at other suspected crash sites in the Roswell area. There was even a section devoted to film that included an alien prop donated by Paul Davids, the producer and director of the 1994 Showtime Original Film *Roswell* starring Martin Sheen.

“Do you want to skip this section?” Roger asked at the entrance to a room near the end of the tour filled with space and alien art.

“Not at all. It might be fun,” Amanda replied. Inside, they were treated to dozens of planetscapes, with titles like ‘The Moons of Tiron 4’ and artist interpretations of the first alien-earthling encounters. Most of the items were priced for sale. A woman with a young child in a stroller was admiring a foot-high green-glazed piece depicting a pair of aliens in embrace. Her husband stood a safe distance away, arms folded.

Roger and Amanda couldn’t help but hear the woman. “I think we should get it, Jerry. It’s only two-hundred-and-fifty dollars.”

“We have to leave,” the husband declared impatiently.

Roger and Amanda stepped quietly past the couple. A cashier up ahead was busy behind a counter at the archway that led back to the entrance lobby where the tour had begun. She handed a teenage boy a bag containing the alien calendar he had picked out and thanked him for his purchase. She smiled broadly as Amanda and Roger approached.

“Did you folks enjoy your tour today?” she asked.

“Very much,” Amanda answered. Roger nodded in agreement.

“Wouldn’t you like to take home a souvenir of your visit? We have some wonderful books and postcards and gifts. If you have young children, we have alien coloring books and—”

“No thank you,” Amanda interrupted. “But can you tell us where we might find some background history about the town, particularly from the 1940s?”

“Well—your best bet would be the historical society. It’s only a half mile from here, but they are closed for the holiday, until after New Year’s. Have you tried the public library?”

“Yes, we have.”

“Our library, here at the Museum, has some material on city history. I know we have a good photo collection of Roswell and the surrounding area; much of it from the war years, I believe.”

“We must have missed it,” offered Roger.

“It’s not part of the regular tour, mainly it’s for researchers. Just go back to the lobby where the tour starts; someone can direct you to the Research Center Library.”

ROGER AND AMANDA were greeted by the Museum Curator in the library. After introductions, he asked, "What can I help you with, Professor Atwood?"

"Ms. Marshall and I are working on a research project concerning some of the contractors that were supporting Roswell Army Air Field operations during and after World War Two. We are especially interested in an entity known as The Wormstone Group, or possibly with the name, Wormstone Engineering."

Amanda added, "We believe the company was founded here in 1944."

"The name isn't familiar, but there might be some reference to the company in one of these volumes." He pointed at the full shelves of books. "I haven't read everything in this room. But the material here is organized by subject, not chronology. It might be hard to find."

"What about your photo collection?"

"Now that might help you. Most of the photos are well-documented and are generally arranged chronologically."

"Where do we start?" Amanda asked.

THE RESEARCH CENTER PHOTO COLLECTION available to both amateur and professional investigators—and virtually anyone else who could come up with a plausible rationale to see it—was stored in a bank of common letter-size file cabinets. Each photo was a copy or enlargement of the original, printed on glossy eight-by-ten photographic paper and placed in a celluloid sleeve. The back of each print was marked with an index number, identifying it uniquely in the computerized database that included a description of the object or event depicted in the photo, the date—if known—when the photograph was taken, the ID number of the original negative or print stored in a secure location off-site, and the source; that is, how the museum came to acquire the photo.

The curator was displaying the contents of the database file on one of the library workstations. "The description field shown here in the database table is also printed on the reverse side of each print. And while you can see a field labeled 'Image' in the table, you won't find any images there. We just now started creating high resolution j-peg copies of all of our original prints, slides and negatives. Eventually, we'll be able to dispose of the hard copies in these file cabinets." He scrolled down to the last record in the table and announced proudly, "We have 2,752 photos in the collection, as of today."

"Can we do a word search on the description field?" Roger asked.

"Of course. Should I search for the word 'Wormstone'?" Roger nodded in the affirmative. It took only a second for the workstation to display the message, 'No records found'.

"That's too bad," offered Amanda. "But we'd still like to look through your collection of prints."

They started with the first of three file cabinet drawers labeled 'Roswell and Vicinity — War Years'. But it wasn't long before it became clear that the Curator's earlier glowing claims of a structured organization for the photo collection were somewhat exaggerated. The chronology seemed haphazard, with the first drawer containing a sequence of declassified government photos of the first atomic bomb test at Trinity Site in Alamogordo in 1945, just before the end of the war. And nearly half of the photos they examined had no description whatsoever.

The photographs, although interesting, provided no help to Roger and Amanda in their search for information concerning Wormstone Engineering. That is, until Roger flipped past a photograph near the middle of a set of photos from the third drawer.

"Go back one, Roger." He obliged. "This is the same photo I told you about—the one in the conference room at the Wormstone Group in Virginia." She turned the photo over to read the description:

COMPANY FOUNDER, DR. THOMAS STARK (LEFT), FORMERLY OF BELL LABORATORIES, AT GROUND BREAKING CEREMONY FOR WORM STONE ENGINEERING ROSWELL FACILITY, APRIL 10, 1944.

"So why didn't the search for 'Wormstone' in the database file catch this record?" She asked.

The Curator was working nearby and heard Amanda's question. He came over to examine the photograph and the text printed on the back. "That's easy," he said. "We searched for the single word, 'Wormstone', not two separate words, 'Worm' and 'Stone'. The computer is pretty fickle that way. If the text in the record is not spelled exactly the same as the search term, it won't find anything. The company name was simply entered incorrectly in the database."

"So how can we find this place?" Roger asked. "Can you tell anything from the photo?" The Curator removed his eyeglasses and brought the photograph very close—only inches from his nose.

"I know about where this was taken." Roger and Amanda's attention was focused on the Curator's words. "You see the pylon in the background?" They nodded. "There was one on the approach to the airfield main runway to give pilots an indication of wind direction and warn of cross winds. This photo was probably taken somewhere on Y.O. Road. You'll find it on the south side of the airport."

CHAPTER NINE

JANUARY 1982. The United States was in the midst of a deep recession. High interest rates were the prescribed cure for the runaway inflation that had gripped the country during the Ford and Carter administrations, and the cure had nearly killed the patient. Ronald Reagan had been in office for just one year, and although there were some hopeful signs of recovery, the economy was still under pressure. Unemployment continued to rise and wouldn't begin to level off until reaching nearly eleven percent later in the year. In the City of Las Vegas, conditions were especially grim. It had all started six years earlier when gambling was legalized in Atlantic City, New Jersey. The westward flow of east coast vacationers, once eager to take their chances at what had been the only legalized gaming tables in the country, was reduced to a trickle nearly overnight; then further reduced to a mere drip after the Iranian Revolution of 1979 and the accompanying spike in fuel prices.

In 1977, the City lost its biggest entertainment drawing card with the death of Elvis Presley in Memphis on August 17th. And even international visitors began to reconsider their travel plans when in November 1980 the MGM Grand Hotel on the Las Vegas Strip burned with the loss of seventy-seven lives. Less than three months later an arson fire at the Las Vegas Hilton killed eight more. But for those residents of the City and surrounding towns who still had jobs and money to spend, the casinos of Las Vegas were high on the list of popular fun stops. The inexpensive rooms and meals, no crowds, great entertainment and looser-than-usual slots attracted more locals as well as visitors from nearby towns in Southern Nevada, Arizona and Southern California.

WILLIAM EVERETT ADAMS worked in Groom Lake, Nevada, one hundred and fifty miles northwest of Las Vegas. He was a test pilot for Lockheed Aircraft Corporation, twenty-six years old, single and enjoying life. He had joined Lockheed after four years in the Air Force and had recently moved from Texas. The new job was stressful, with long hours during the week, but flight operations ended early on Fridays. There were virtually no weekend social activities for unmarried contractor and military personnel in Groom Lake. Consequently, Ev Adams and most of his single coworkers looked forward to spending weekends in nearby Las Vegas.

Ev was proud of his new yellow ragtop Corvette and bragged that he could get from the Main Gate at the base to the Las Vegas city limit sign in two hours flat. He usually drove alone as his occasional passenger generally found the ride a bit too exhilarating. Ev appreciated fast cars, planes and women. He didn't smoke, and drank only moderately. In fact, William Everett Adams had never dealt with addictions of any kind. That is, not until he moved to Nevada.

CHAPTER TEN

Y.O. ROAD WAS EASY TO FIND. It skirted the entire south side of the Roswell International Air Center Airport, formerly the Roswell Army Air Field. Roger slowly cruised the length of the road from west to east, then turned around and headed back in the opposite direction. The airfield was now visible outside the passenger window of the Jeep.

"It's a good thing this town's economy is pumped up by the UFO tourists. Not much business activity in this part of town." Amanda was commenting on the number vacant buildings they found along Y.O. Road. They passed a few open machine shops and auto repair businesses, and even an aircraft maintenance facility that appeared to be open, but most of the businesses seemed to be surviving rather than prospering. Many hadn't been painted in years and weeds were growing out of the cracks in the asphalt parking lots.

Amanda kept comparing the background in the copy of the photo from the UFO Research Center with the view outside the Jeep's passenger window. "It looks to me that the Wormstone facility must have been somewhere nearby. We're close; slow down a little." Roger slowed the vehicle and pulled closer to the gravel shoulder of the roadway.

“Did you see that?” Roger exclaimed.

“No, what?” The Jeep was now directly in front of the first of four adjacent abandoned buildings.

“Behind this building.” Roger shifted into reverse and backed the Jeep about fifty feet. “There.” He pointed. “Check out the truck—under that tarp.” Roger pulled forward and turned into the driveway that ran along the side of the building and parked. “Let’s take a closer look.”

As they approached the truck, Amanda remarked, “It’s the right color.” Roger lifted the tarp at the right rear fender near the bumper, revealing the scratched and dented body panel. But it was the blue paint residue on the fender that made it clear that this was indeed the truck that sideswiped them on Route 285 on their way into Roswell. Roger ran back toward the Jeep.

“What are you doing, Roger?”

“I want to see if we can get inside this building, but I don’t want to attract any attention.” Roger pulled the Jeep behind the building, effectively concealing their presence from anyone who might be driving along Y.O. Road.

There were not a lot of options. The short row of high windows above them was simply out of reach, but they afforded some view of the interior of the building. Inside they could see the high ceiling of the large bay making up the rear half of the building. An interior wall ran the full length of the bay. Near the end of the row of windows and below them was a solid door. It was locked.

“Look at this sticker.” It was faded—barely legible, but they could read it:

DELIVERIES AFTER 4PM REQUIRE PRIOR AUTHORIZATION. CONTACT WORMSTONE SHIPPING/RECEIVING (702) 555-8787 EXT 212.

This was the place! Roger tried to push up on the two steel rollup doors further along the rear wall, but neither budged more than an inch. These doors typically opened only from the inside by drawing on a heavy chain that turned the rollup mechanism at the top of each door. Around the corner Roger found another standard door. He pulled on the handle, expecting it to be locked, but was surprised to find that it opened easily. Roger called to Amanda and the two of them slipped inside the building.

The large bay was well lit thanks to the light entering from the row of high windows and some scattered skylights in the high ceiling. It was dirty inside, and empty. Some faded posters on the walls cautioned about such things as wearing adequate eye protection and other safe working practices including a warning to report all work injuries to a supervisor. Clearly they were in some sort of shop or assembly area. Two parallel corridors led forward from the bay to a half-dozen offices and a lobby beyond with the main entrance at the front of the building. All of the unlocked doors led to empty office spaces—not even a stick of furniture. But the door marked PERSONNEL OFFICE was locked.

"What do you think?" asked Roger. "We could already be charged with trespassing. Should I kick it in?" Amanda nodded. It took three tries, but the door finally flew open. It was dark inside—the only light coming in from the open doorway—but they could see a pair of four-drawer filing cabinets against the far wall. The file cabinet on the left had a large placard attached to the front of the top drawer that read CONFIDENTIAL. There was a hasp at the top of the cabinet and a bar that ran to the bottom—capable of securing all of the drawers—but there was no lock. When Roger removed the bar, he was able to open the file drawers. Every one was empty. The placard on the other file cabinet read UNCLASSIFIED MATERIAL. From it, Roger and Amanda each took an armful of file folders out into the hallway where the light was better and began leafing through documents.

What they found were contracts—copies of government contracts going back to 1944. There were contracts for all manner of support to the airbase, from refurbishing radio electronics to supporting the deactivation of Atlas missile silos nearby.

"I don't understand." Amanda stopped reading for a moment and looked at Roger, "I see a lot of early contracts with Roswell Army Air Field, but why are there so many from Walker Air Force Base? Was the Wormstone facility here in Roswell working for the Walker Base as well?"

"I can answer that," offered Roger. "It's the same place. When the Air Force took over, they renamed it in honor of a hero airman from World War Two. I can tell you more about it, if you'd like to hear it."

"Why do I have the feeling that you're going to tell me, whether or not I want to hear it? Sure. Go ahead."

"It's pretty interesting, honest, but I'll give you the abridged version. Walker—his first name was

Kenneth—was a career Army Air Corps officer when the Japanese attacked Pearl Harbor. Six months later he was promoted to Brigadier General and sent to the Pacific as head of a bomber command. The General personally led several bombing missions over Rabaul in New Britain that was held by the Japanese. On one of these missions in early 1943 his B-17 was shot down. His body was never recovered and he was awarded the Medal of Honor posthumously by President Roosevelt. He was from New Mexico, which is why the air base was named in his honor."

"Very interesting, Roger, but please tell me why we are looking at all these contracts? They're awfully boring and not telling us anything."

"You're right." Roger tossed the contract he had been examining to the floor and went back to retrieve the last few folders remaining in the file cabinet. Returning to the hallway, he handed half of them to Amanda and sat with his back propped against the hallway wall as he leafed through the pages.

The second group of file folders contained mainly employment-related documents. They found old job applications, performance reviews and pay records for Wormstone's hourly and salaried employees. One thick folder examined by Amanda was labeled "Exit Interviews" and contained employee separation records. Included was a batch of about twenty, all with the same termination date, June 30th 1967. The "Reason for Separation" was shown as "Base Closure." Further into the stack she found separation records dated much earlier. "This is interesting, Roger. Some of these folks apparently were asked to sign a non-disclosure pledge concerning the 1947 UFO incident."

"Really? Let me see." Roger stretched out his arm and Amanda passed him one of the papers. Roger read the short text of the pledge statement to himself:

> I UNDERSTAND THAT I MAY NOT DISCLOSE INFORMATION ABOUT EVENTS FOR WHICH I MAY HAVE DIRECT OR INDIRECT KNOWLEDGE CONCERNING THE ALLEGED CRASH OF A FLYING OBJECT NEAR ROSWELL, NEW MEXICO, WHICH MAY HAVE OCCURRED SOMETIME DURING THE MONTH OF JULY 1947. I UNDERSTAND THAT SUCH DISCLOSURE, OR ANY AFFIRMING ACKNOWLEDGEMENT OF THE DISCLOSURE OF SAME BY OTHERS, CONSTITUTES A VIOLATION OF THE SECURITY LAWS OF THE UNITED STATES AND IS PUNISHABLE BY FINES AND IMPRISONMENT.

There was a line below the statement for the employee to sign and enter the date. "That's a pretty heavy warning, don't you think? From these records, it looks as if anyone who was employed prior to July 1947 had to sign the pledge," Amanda added. She continued to peruse the documents, in order to confirm her conclusion. Minutes later, she was startled to find a particular name among those who had signed the non-disclosure pledge. "Roger. . . ."

"Yes?"

"Would you look in your stack of employment records for the name 'Marjorie Hedrick'? A woman by that name signed the non-disclosure pledge in June 1951."

Roger shuffled through the employment records in the pile in front of him. When he found the original application for employment from Marjorie Hedrick, submitted in February 1946, he began to read the details aloud. "Listen to this: Marjorie Hedrick, born January 15, 1927. Place of Birth: Des Moines, Iowa. Marital Status: Married. Spouse's Name: Dieter Hedrick, Lieutenant RAAF." He paused. "Did your Dieter happen to mention that his wife worked for Wormstone?"

"No, he didn't have time to tell me much of anything about his personal life."

CHAPTER ELEVEN

EXCEPT FOR THE DEALER, the participants in the poker game in the suite at the Sands Hotel had left the table for the previously-agreed-upon fifteen minute break at midnight. Ev Adams joined Anthony Costello, a coworker—also a player at the poker table—at the corner window of the tower suite. Costello lit a cigarette; Ev Adams sipped from the fresh tumbler of Tanqueray on the rocks that had been delivered minutes earlier by the busty blonde server assigned to their table for the evening.

The view from the suite was impressive. Directly across Las Vegas Boulevard stood the New Frontier Hotel and next to it on the north side, the Silver Slipper. The view to the south included the rear portion of Caesar's Palace and immediately adjacent to their hotel, across Sands Avenue, was the Desert Inn. "Don't you think we should be leaving, Ev?" Everett Adams made no reply to the question. Anthony continued, "That radar signature test starts at eight in the morning." Costello was tired and wanted to head back to Groom Lake.

"Easy for you to say. You're up a few hundred; I'm down more than a thou'."

"C'mon. You can make it up next weekend."

“Just a couple more hands, then we’ll go. I promise.”

When play resumed back at the table, Ev and Anthony learned that two of the seven starters from earlier that evening had cashed in their chips and left the suite. Besides Ev and Anthony, that left only Stefan, the owner of a local independent European auto service business, Texas Joe Holcomb, an oilman on vacation in the city with his family, and a Russian building contractor, known to the group simply as “Leo the Russian.”

Texas Joe won the first hand of seven card stud after the break. His last hole card completed a Jack-high straight, beating Ev’s three Kings. The other three players had folded before the last card was dealt. After the dealer counted out the three percent cut for the house, Texas Joe collected a one-hundred and twenty-five dollar pot. In the second hand, the Russian initiated the betting at forty dollars on his pair of queens in the hole, showing a three of clubs face up. Anthony folded. Stefan called with a low pair; ditto for Texas Joe. Ev held two small clubs and a third face up—a possible straight flush—and called also. By the time the last face up card was dealt, Stefan was out. The Russian had drawn another three, now holding two pair. Ev drew another club—his forth—and had a pair of sevens up. Texas Joe checked his pair of tens showing and now held two pair. Ev checked as well, but the Russian bet eighty dollars, and Texas Joe and Ev called. The dealer dealt the last card to the three remaining players. The Russian bet the limit—one hundred dollars. Texas Joe didn’t improve his hand and folded. Ev had drawn a fifth club and raised another hundred. The Russian immediately raised back and Ev finally called. But the eleven hundred dollar pot went to the Russian, having drawn a third queen, making his full house and beating Ev's flush.

"Let's get the hell out of here." Everett Adams was disgusted. He had lost nearly two thousand dollars in the last four hours of play. They quickly cashed in and Anthony tipped the dealer twenty dollars; Ev gave him nothing.

"See you here next Sunday, gentlemen?" The Russian called out to the pair. Anthony Costello turned and returned a shrug. Ev Adams ignored the question. They left the suite and headed back to Groom Lake.

There was little communication between the two men on the ride back to the base. Upset over his losses, Ev didn't feel like talking. Anthony Costello took advantage of the quiet time by napping. He awoke just as Ev pulled up to the main gate—the only one open at that hour. It was after two AM. The guard recognized the pair as cleared employees and waved them in without checking identification. They might just get four hours of sleep before having to be up and showered, fed and on the flight line for the morning radar tests.

BY EARLY 1982, Lockheed production of the F-117 Nighthawk—also known as the Stealth Fighter—was underway. The very existence of this aircraft was a well-kept secret. The secrecy had little to do with its speed or payload. What made this aircraft special was the fact it was virtually invisible to most of the world's known radar systems.

The basic design principle was rather simple. Radar works by transmitting radio frequency electromagnetic wave pulses in the direction from which target aircraft may be approaching. Upon striking a target aircraft, some of the radar energy is reflected back to the radar unit where a receiver detects and amplifies the return signal. By determining the direction from which the return is coming and the elapsed time between the transmission of a pulse and receipt of the return signal, it is possible to determine both the angular direction to the target and its distance. In stealth aircraft design, the surfaces struck by the transmitted waves are generally flat and angled in such a way that the radar waves impinging upon the target are reflected in a direction away from the radar system, so that there is little or no return for the receiver to detect, making the target effectively invisible. Detectability may be further reduced by employing special paints or radar absorbing materials in the design.

ONE OF THE PARAMETERS used to measure stealth performance is Radar Cross-Section, or RCS. It is a measure of how detectable an object such as an airplane will be. For example, an aircraft with a one square meter RCS value would have the same approximate degree of visibility to a radar system as a metal sphere of size that would cast a shadow one square meter in area. A truly stealthy aircraft might have an RCS value of a few hundredths of a square meter. One current stealth design is said to achieve the same degree of radar (in)visibility as a steel ball bearing the size of a marble. But assuring that minimal reflected energy is returned back to the radar receiver makes for difficult aircraft design. Jet engines need to breathe, and so there must be an intake of sorts with a shape that is likely to reflect some radar energy back to the source. And bombs and missiles cannot be hung below the wings as with a conventional air frame; they need to be carried internally lest they add to the overall radar return. Finally, the faceted shape of the body and severely swept back wings—features that optimize stealth characteristics—make for an aircraft with grave inherent instability. Control surfaces on such an aircraft must be computer-actuated to be able to respond to continuous corrections in real time in order to simply maintain level flight.

Although the Air Force had begun taking delivery of their new fighter only months earlier, several new sole source contracts had already been awarded to the Skunkworks at Lockheed to further improve both the performance and stealth characteristics of the Nighthawk. Everett Adams and a select few other Skunkworks test pilots had the task of helping to determine the effectiveness of the engineering changes proposed by Lockheed's design engineers.

"WHAT'S WITH THE NEW PAINT JOB?" Ev was performing an exterior inspection of the F-117A test bed aircraft he had flown nearly every week day in the last month. It was part of his usual pre-flight check.

"Pretty weird, huh?" The flight line technician took notes on his clipboard as Ev called out a few minor concerns. "It's called Ironball. They use it on the Blackbird. It's 'sposed to contain little iron spheres that are coated with some exotic shit. Theory is that some of the radar energy gets converted to heat so there's less of it to get reflected back to the source."

"Does it work?"

"I guess that's what we're going to find out today."

CHAPTER TWELVE

THE NUMBER OF HOUSES AND RANCHES along West Pine Lodge Road appeared to vary inversely with their distance from town. And so the home address listed on Marjorie Hedrick's application for employment at Wormstone Engineering—some twenty miles from the center of Roswell—was easy to find. Roger and Amanda had just about zero expectation that anyone would still be living at the same address after fifty plus years, especially after observing how desolate and inhospitable the land appeared. And so as they turned into the gravel driveway, they were pleasantly surprised to find the name 'Hedrick' on the mailbox.

"This may be our lucky day, Amanda," Roger remarked as they approached the front door of the old single story ranch style home. Amanda had no comment.

The woman who answered the door appeared to be in her late seventies, short gray hair and slightly heavy for her height. "Can I help you folks?"

"Mrs. Hedrick, is it?" Roger asked.

"Yes—"

"My name is Roger Atwood and this is Amanda Marshall." Not knowing if she was aware of her husband's passing, Roger was unsure just how to proceed with Mrs. Hedrick. After a glance at Amanda, he decided on a neutral approach. "We came here today to inquire about your husband, Colonel Dieter Hedrick."

A male voice called out from somewhere in the back of the home, "Who is it, Marjorie?"

Marjorie called back to the voice, "Just a couple here, who know Dieter." No response from the back room. "Why don't you folks come in?"

The living room furniture looked as if it had come out of a time capsule—crocheted doilies pinned to the arms of the sofa and beige throws with an edge fringe of tassels draping the two overstuffed chairs down to the dark stained wood claw foot legs. The large oval braided rug covering most of the hardwood floor was well worn. Mrs. Hedrick invited her visitors to be seated on the sofa.

"Dieter is my ex-husband. We were divorced some fifty years ago. It's been a long time since we've spoken."

"Actually, Mrs. Hedrick, we are sorry to bring you the news that your ex-husband passed away in New York a month ago."

Marjorie lowered her head and looked down at her hands clasped loosely together in her lap. "I guess I shouldn't be surprised—the years just slip away, don't they? But Dieter was always pretty health conscious. I figured he'd outlive me. He even quit cigarettes long before all the warnings about smoking and health came out. How did he—I mean, what can you tell me about his passing?"

"Colonel Hedrick was hospitalized in New York for a terminal illness. I don't know what medical condition he was suffering from, but the police have ruled his death a homicide. He was murdered. I'm so sorry," Amanda added. The expression of pain on Marjorie Hedrick's face quickly turned to shock and she began to weep.

"Dieter was a good man." She paused. "I think I need a cup of tea. Can I offer you some?"

"That would be nice," replied Amanda. Marjorie disappeared for a few minutes and returned with a tray with four cups of tea. As Amanda and Roger watched her place three cups on the glass top of the coffee table, it was apparent to both of them that Mrs. Hedrick had been shaken by the news of her ex-husband's death.

"I'll be back in a minute," she said. "I want to take some tea to my brother."

When she returned to her visitors in the living room, Marjorie Hedrick was somewhat more composed. She lowered her voice as she spoke. "I'm sorry. My brother's not doing too well these days. And the news about Dieter was hard to hear. I'm feeling better now." She paused before continuing. "You knew Dieter? Were you related?"

"No, ma'am."

"Dieter told you about me then? And asked you to come here?"

"No, ma'am, not exactly." Amanda was answering the questions now.

"Tell me again, why is it that you came here?"

"Let me explain, Mrs. Hedrick. I'm a journalist and I was interviewing your ex-husband before he passed away concerning his knowledge of the Roswell UFO incident."

"You want to write another story about the UFO incident? Is there anything new that hasn't already been written?" Marjorie didn't wait for an answer. "Well, Dieter was certainly the man to ask. He was right in the middle of it all." She paused before continuing. "And Dieter didn't tell you about me? Is that what you said?"

Now Roger took the lead. "That's correct, ma'am. While doing some research, we learned that at one time you worked for one of the base contractors."

"Yes. I worked for Wormstone Engineering for three years while Dieter and I were married. Then we separated when they transferred him to Lackland in Texas. I didn't go with him; the marriage was pretty much over by then. Dieter was a good man but I guess I couldn't accept always being second to his career. I worked at Wormstone for two more years before I quit."

"We found out that you and many other Wormstone people signed a non-disclosure pledge, agreeing not to disclose anything you might know about the UFO incident."

"Sure, I still remember that damn form. They made me sign it on my last day at work; wouldn't give me my final paycheck until I did."

"Then it is true? You were privy to information concerning the events of July 1947 that the government wanted to keep quiet?"

Marjorie drew one hand up to her chin and mouth. "I – I don't know that I should be talking about this. I promised that I wouldn't." Roger had a quizzical expression on his face. She had promised—who? "You know, that non-disclosure form. I signed it, promising not to talk about the incident—anything that I knew or had heard about the crash."

"I'm sure that the government isn't too concerned about people disclosing events that occurred more than fifty years ago." Roger was trying to sound convincing, without being condescending. "Besides, the Air Force declassified all their official documents concerning Roswell years ago."

"I suppose you're right, Mr. Atwood. You know, my ex-husband told me a lot that he probably should have kept to himself. But those stories about injured or dead aliens being recovered—they simply weren't true."

"And you know this because . . .?"

"Because Dieter was in charge of the recovery operation, and according to him, there were no aliens found, dead or alive. My memory is still pretty good, and I remember the whole story, just as he told it. It's hard to believe so many years have passed."

CHAPTER THIRTEEN

"WHAT THE HELL, LIEUTENANT? Why didn't you tell me we were headed to another crash site?" Sergeant Whittaker was the driver of one of two flat bed trucks in the procession of Army vehicles on a dirt road somewhere southeast of Corona, New Mexico.

His passenger, Lieutenant Dieter Hedrick, took one last hit from his cigarette before extinguishing it and then answered the Sergeant. "Did you think we were going to a Boy Scout Jamboree? The Colonel put a tight lid on this, just like when we picked up all that balloon wreckage last week." Dieter Hedrick was referring to the recovery operation initiated as a result of Mac Brazel's discovery of the balloon debris in the desert a week earlier, on July 3, 1947.

The small convoy included a Jeep at the point and one following behind. The second flatbed carried a loader. The recovery team had left Roswell Army Air Field that morning at dawn and proceeded to the northwest. Although only some forty miles from the base as the crow flies, they had been on the road for hours, mainly due to confusion about the exact crash site location. It had been first reported incorrectly by the officer sent to investigate the day before. The initial account came from two local ranchers who saw a flying object come down at a high angle and crash in the desert. Dieter Hedrick's Army map of the area was pretty primitive and it took a radio call to the reporting officer before the recovery team got on the right dirt road leading to the crash site.

Lieutenant Hedrick climbed down from the truck cab and evaluated the extent of the debris field. "Have the men set up camp." He lit another cigarette. "We're going to be here for another day or two."

Sergeant Whittaker relayed the order to the dozen other enlisted men in the recovery team, and then rejoined Lieutenant Hedrick as he surveyed the wreckage. Pieces of the craft were strewn over an area at least two hundred yards long and fifty yards wide. There were three pieces of wreckage large enough to require the loader plus a lot of small broken metal parts—many with strands of wire attached—and more than a hundred pieces of what appeared to be the skin of the object—some unknown thin black material with no hint of markings whatsoever. Many of the pieces showed evidence of an explosion and fire.

"Do you think this was one of them flying saucers—from outer space?" Sergeant Whittaker was referring to the press release from the Roswell Information Office that initially reported that personnel from the 509th Bomb Group at the Roswell Army Air Field (RAAF) had recovered a crashed "flying disc" from a ranch near town.

There was an official retraction later that day and a subsequent press conference that claimed that the downed object was in fact a weather balloon, but not before the story was picked up by the local newspaper. Headlines in *The Roswell Daily Record* of Tuesday, July 8, 1947 announced to the world, "RAAF CAPTURES FLYING SAUCER ON RANCH IN ROSWELL REGION."

Dieter Hedrick simply shrugged. "Who knows? It's going to take someone a helluva lot smarter than us to figure out what this son-of-a-bitch looked like before it crashed." He returned to the truck to retrieve a clipboard and proceeded to sketch out the relative fallen positions of the largest pieces of debris. It might help the reconstruction team in their work. By the time he had finished the sketch, the camp setup was complete and he called the enlisted team together for an impromptu meeting.

"Listen up, men." He paused until he had everyone's attention. "You've heard the rumors—about all the sightings of flying discs by the locals in the last month or two. Plus the newspaper accounts after that first press release from the base. I don't know what we have here. Could be German. We pulled a whole shitload of Nazi experimental aircraft out of secret caves under the Harz Mountains just before the Russians got there. Then again, it could be aliens." One of the privates was fidgeting, then raised his hand. "What is it, Perkins?"

"You said aliens, sir. You mean—like—from Mexico?" Sergeant Whittaker began to laugh. Dieter Hedrick wasn't laughing.

"No, Perkins. I mean aliens, like from another planet. One thing's for certain: I haven't seen anything here that looks like it was made in the USA. What I want you all to do is to pay attention during the recovery work. Look out for any clues as to where this thing is from. And if you find any organic matter—that means any body parts, Perkins—give a shout out immediately. Now, get back to work. You're all dismissed."

The crew spent the rest of the afternoon picking up the parts that were strewn across the New Mexico desert. Loose pieces of the black skin material went in one large crate. Anything that looked electrical—or electronic—went in another. Other miscellaneous small parts went in a third crate. The crew knocked off work at 5 PM; the largest sections of the craft would be left for morning and the loader.

Dinner for the officer and his men that evening consisted of K-Rations. Tonight it would be canned pork luncheon meat, biscuits, a chocolate bar and an after-dinner pack of four cigarettes. The only thing that was hot was the coffee brewed on the campfire. Sergeant Whittaker finished his meal, poured another cup of coffee into the tin cup from his mess kit and lit a cigarette. He sat by the fire, next to Lieutenant Hedrick.

"Do you mind if I ask you a question, sir?"

"Not at all, Sergeant."

"Why do you think there have been so many reported sightings lately? I mean, from civilians."

Lieutenant Hedrick poked at the campfire with a stick as he considered Sergeant Whittaker's question. "You must have noticed that we've had a general increase in the amount of air traffic around the base in the last few weeks; maybe twice as much as six months ago. Stands to reason that we'd get more civilians reporting stuff they perceive as unusual. Might not be unusual at all. Maybe it's one of those captured Nazi jets, or maybe even one of ours that flew up from White Sands."

THE RECOVERY TEAM finished their work the next morning. First on the agenda was moving the three largest pieces of crash wreckage on to the flat beds. The two largest were loaded on one of the trucks; the smallest on the second flat bed, allowing room for the loader itself. Then Lieutenant Hedrick ordered the enlisted personnel to line up at the inbound edge of the debris field and make one last pass over the area in search of smaller items that might have been missed. The men stayed in a single side-by-side line—four feet apart—advancing slowly over the area; each man concentrating on the four-foot width of ground immediately ahead of him. Two men followed behind pulling a wagon fitted with rubber tires to collect the items spotted and picked up by the advancing line up ahead. When they reached the end of the debris field, the line turned about to cover the adjacent width of ground. This was repeated a half-dozen times, until the full width of the debris field was thoroughly searched. When they were done, they had filled the wagon with a mix of small items from the crash.

The recovery convoy was back on the road to Roswell shortly after noon. Lieutenant Hedrick made a preliminary report of his findings by radio. Colonel

Blanchard, the base commander, called him back an hour later with new orders. “By the time you get back to base, a cargo plane will be on the flight line waiting to take the crate of electronic stuff to Wright-Pat. Everything else goes to Wormstone Engineering, just south of the base on Y.O. Road. You know where it is?”

“Of course, sir.”

CHAPTER FOURTEEN

AFTER RELATING HER EX-HUSBAND'S account of the work of the recovery team at the crash site, Marjorie Hedrick excused herself briefly and then returned to the living room with more hot tea and some sugar cookies. Roger had some questions.

"Were you working at Wormstone that day when the parts from the crash were brought in?"

"Yes, I was."

"What can you tell us about that day? What did you see?"

"Not a great deal. The military kept most of us from getting too close—plenty of guards and everything under wraps. They took the wreckage into the building next door. This was a bit of a surprise to me since I knew there was an operating auto repair business in that building. I had spoken to the owner earlier in the week about getting the brakes fixed on our car.

When I asked Dieter about it that night at home, he said that the Army had come in the night before and kicked the owner out. They paid him off, towed away all the cars that were in for repair and cleared the building of everything but the tools. Dieter told me that some men from the base and a couple of Wormstone engineers with top secret clearances spent the next several months trying to reassemble the wreckage from the crash."

"This work was going on in the building immediately adjacent to Wormstone's main facility—the one out on Y.O. Road?"

"Yes. We called it the Wormstone Annex."

"And were they able to finish the job?"

"I don't know. After a few days Dieter became pretty close-mouthed about the work going on there. But they must have had problems because it wasn't long before the Army brought in a lot of scientists from Wright-Patterson and Bell Laboratories. I know because I saw the visitor log books."

BELL LABORATORIES WAS ORGANIZED in 1925 as a consolidation of research and engineering department personnel from Western Electric and American Telephone and Telegraph. Much of the early work of this preeminent research organization was devoted to developing telephone system hardware and documenting best practices for telephone installation and service. But as their reputation for technical excellence grew, the scientists at Bell Labs began to do more basic research, much of which was conducted under government research contracts. The laboratory pioneered work in such diverse fields as radio astronomy, television, and statistical process control theory for quality assurance.

It was not considered unusual, then, when a crate of strange looking electrical parts from Hangar 18 at Wright-Patterson Field arrived at Bell Labs in Murray Hill, New Jersey, in mid July 1947. During the telephone call from the government sponsor in Ohio, the Bell Labs Project Manager was told that the parts were sent with the expectation that they might help laboratory personnel with an old and ongoing project of finding substitute technology for the amplifier and switch circuits currently designed using vacuum tubes. Vacuum tubes were bulky, consumed a lot of power, were slow in switching applications and considered insufficiently reliable for projects on the drawing board that could conceivably require thousands of such devices. When asked about the source of the parts, the government sponsor reluctantly conceded that they may have originally come from Germany—or maybe not.

Work of the research group immediately began in earnest. Two teams of scientists and assisting technicians were organized to learn what they could from the cache of miscellaneous parts. One team was assigned the task of determining macro characteristics. That is, what were the physical properties of the parts, what function did they perform and how did they respond to different sorts of stimulation, including electrical, chemical, light and sound? The second team was tasked with determining the microstructure and makeup of the active elements within the parts.

Within a few weeks, some startling discoveries were made. The macro team learned that by applying low voltages to specific electrical contacts, they could duplicate the behavior of common vacuum tube circuits designed for amplification and triggering. Meanwhile, the micro group observed that what often appeared as a single component to the unaided eye revealed hundreds of tiny active elements when subjected to the ultra high magnification of the lab's electron microscope.

The macro team also used a mass spectrometer to identify the elemental composition of the components. Repetitive tests confirmed that there were two main classes of objects. The most common consisted of nearly pure silicon, while another group was made up of just as pure germanium crystals. The research group was particularly interested in the germanium components because of the lab's prior success in growing the crystals and using the germanium material in the fabrication of diodes. But it was clear that the components from the Wright-Patterson crate of parts were far more sophisticated than anything developed at Bell Labs by 1947. One researcher remarked, "It's a good thing we beat those Nazi bastards when we did. Given another year or two, who knows what kind of weapons they could have unleashed on us!"

By December 1947, the research team was able to construct for the very first time an operating solid state transistor, leading the way to the huge advances in microelectronics that continued far into the future. But it would be nine years before the world would recognize the importance of this achievement. In 1956 Bell Labs researchers John Bardeen, Walter H. Brattain, and William B. Shockley were awarded the Nobel Prize in Physics for their semiconductor research work and discovery of the transistor effect.

CHAPTER FIFTEEN

EV AND ANTHONY'S WEEKENDS in Las Vegas continued unabated, but by early March 1982 they no longer played together in the same Sands game. Anthony had developed an affinity for craps, at which he played well and usually came out a winner, and roulette which usually took all of his winnings from craps. But for Anthony Costello, gambling was just entertainment. He took neither his wins nor losses very seriously. By contrast, gambling for Everett Adams had developed into an addiction. He had "graduated" from the hundred dollar limit game that he and Anthony were playing together to a table stakes game with a ten-thousand dollar buy-in.

"I've never had such a long losing streak, Leo." Ev and the Russian sat at the bar in the casino at the Sands, getting a bite to eat during a ninety minute dinner break in their poker game.

"Not to worry, my friend. You play well; your luck must change soon."

"Yeah, well, not if I run out of money first!"

"What? You are big, important pilot for big, important government contractor. You must make big paycheck."

"Not that big, Leo."

The Russian reached into his inside jacket pocket and pulled out a checkbook as he turned toward Everett. "You need a loan? I give you whatever you need." As he reached for the pen in his shirt pocket, Ev stretched an open hand out toward the Russian as if to compel him to put the checkbook away.

"No. No, I couldn't." Ev was insistent.

"As you wish." The Russian turned his head away from Ev and raised his right hand as if he had taken some offense at the rejection of his generous offer. "But know that it is available if you need it."

"Thank you, Leo. I appreciate the offer."

The Russian looked at his watch and announced, "Let us go back upstairs and see if your luck has changed."

BUT EV'S LUCK DIDN'T IMPROVE that evening. And at the game the following week, the Russian advanced Ev ten thousand dollars for the buy-in. Over the next few weeks, Ev Adams managed to make some small gains on a few nights—and some big losses on others. By mid-April, the Russian had advanced Ev more than thirty thousand dollars in total. At the casino bar, the Russian seemed unconcerned over Ev's mounting debt, but Everett Adams was clearly upset.

"I don't know if I can ever pay you back, Leo." The Russian shrugged. Ev continued, "I've got to quit playing—stay out of this town. I'll send you whatever I can out of each paycheck until I've paid you back in full. I promise." The Russian was quiet for a few moments. Then he turned toward Ev and placed his hand on Ev's shoulder.

"You are good man, Everett Adams. I believe your sincerity. But I think I have a better solution for this problem. Listen carefully." The Russian paused briefly as if searching for just the right words. "I have some friends—friends that know a little about your work. I know they would pay handsomely to learn more, to—" the Russian hesitated, "—to examine your airplane." The Russian searched Ev's face for a reaction.

"You mean, some Russian friends?" Leo rocked his head and shoulders from side to side as if weighing the question, but without replying. Everett added, "I couldn't do that. It would be treason."

"Oh, come now. Not really. We all know that stealth technology was a Soviet invention. Your designers have simply taken advantage of prior Soviet work. It would be a fair thing for there to be some—some reciprocal sharing of information."

Ev's gaze was directed at the bottles of scotch, bourbon and gin on the glass shelves on the wall of the bar directly in front of him, but he wasn't focused on any of them. He was thinking. Finally, he asked the question that the Russian was waiting to hear. "How could it work?"

Leo's formerly stern expression gave way to a broad smile. "It would be easy. During one of your routine test flights—maybe to the bombing range at Fallon—you have some intermittent electrical difficulty that you report by radio." Leo paused to light a cigarette and took a deep drag. "Then you lose radio contact temporarily and bring the aircraft down at a remote desert location where my friends are waiting for you. They spend an hour or so examining the aircraft and asking questions. Then they leave the area hours before Air Force Search and Rescue locate you and your airplane, both happily intact."

"Let me consider it, Leo."

The Russian rose from his seat, giving Ev a firm squeeze on the shoulder as he passed behind the flyer and headed out of the bar area. Everett Adams signaled to the bartender to pour another drink. He had some serious thinking to do before retiring to his room. But within a minute or two—even before he had touched his drink—Ev began to feel nauseous. And less than a minute later his head began to ache. It was a migraine, and it was quickly incapacitating him. He nearly fell off his barstool and could do nothing but close his eyes and hold his throbbing head with both hands. The pain was excruciating. But then, as suddenly as it had come upon him, the pain and nausea began to dissipate. Soon he was feeling normal again, as if nothing had happened. The whole episode had consumed barely five minutes. Was it stress from contemplating Leo's proposal? He didn't know. Ev was just glad it had passed.

CHAPTER SIXTEEN

AMANDA AND ROGER had been with Marjorie Hedrick for nearly two hours. Marjorie finally had a chance to ask some questions of her own.

"Has anyone been arrested yet in Dieter's death?"

"No—not yet," replied Amanda. "And I find that disappointing considering that we were able to provide descriptions of the suspects. Plus the police had finger prints and video evidence as well. Do you know anyone who would want to keep your ex-husband from talking about Roswell, especially after all these years?"

"No one I can think of by name. But Dieter knew that he was at risk. He told me so the last time we spoke. Dieter was always a bit of a rebel and he ruffled a lot of military feathers—in Roswell and Washington. Guess that's why he never got promoted to General. Right from the beginning of the Roswell incident, he had some strong opinions about the stories that the Army Air Corps officials put out for public consumption."

"What exactly do you mean, Mrs. Hedrick?"

"Dieter believed that the government purposely leaked false reports to explain away the crash evidence and then created—or at least encouraged—all the rumors that were flying around." Amanda remarked to herself that Mrs. Hedrick's last statement was consistent with what she had heard from Dieter Hedrick before he died. Marjorie continued, "You know, there were plenty of supposed eye witness accounts of spacecraft sightings and alien bodies recovered from the crash site. Who knows what the next new theory will be? Dieter believed that those stories—one after another—were encouraged by the Government in order to draw the public's attention away from the truth."

"That's interesting, Mrs. Hedrick," remarked Amanda. "Colonel Hedrick expressed the same opinion to me. Only he didn't have a chance to tell me more. I don't mean to put words in your mouth, but when you speak of 'the truth', I assume you are referring to what your former husband may have been ready to relate to me before he was killed?" Amanda wanted to clearly understand what Marjorie was hinting at, yet seemed until now reticent to directly divulge.

"Yes. That's right."

"Do you know what Colonel Hedrick was preparing to tell me?"

"Well, yes." Marjorie Hedrick hesitated. "Yes, I believe I do."

Before Marjorie could continue, her name was once again called out from the room in the back and she excused herself. Upon returning to the living room after several minutes she offered an apology to her guests. "I'm sorry, but my brother is having some breathing difficulty, and I need to help him with his oxygen." She remained standing, signaling that the visit was over and that her guests needed to leave.

"Certainly, Mrs. Hedrick. Do you think we could continue this at a later date? Maybe tomorrow or the next day? Could you give us your phone number so that we can call before coming?" Amanda was persistent.

Marjorie scribbled her phone number on a pad of paper from the writing desk behind the sofa. "I suppose that would be all right." She handed the paper to Amanda. "But be sure to call first." With the implicit but abrupt invitation to leave, Amanda Marshall and Roger Atwood left the Hedrick home on West Pine Lodge Road and headed back toward Roswell.

ON THE WAY BACK INTO TOWN, Amanda was the first to bring up the subject they were each thinking about. "It seemed to me that Marjorie was ready to talk until her brother called for her. After that, she couldn't wait for us to leave. What do you think, Roger?"

"Hard to say," offered Roger. "It's pretty clear that the man was ill, or he wouldn't have been holed up in that back room all afternoon. I don't think we can assume that he told her to stop talking to us."

"I disagree. I think that's exactly what happened." Roger simply shrugged at Amanda's comment.

CHAPTER SEVENTEEN

"CAN YOU HELP ME UNDERSTAND this, Ba Noi?" Mai Tran had brought the book to her grandmother's apartment in the Bronx, in the Vietnamese and Cambodian neighborhood of University Heights. The spoken language of her immigrant parents, both now deceased, was no problem for Mai Tran; she was quite fluent. She had no trouble understanding the essence of any family conversation while growing up at home. But having no formal training in the language of her ancestors, printed Vietnamese was often difficult for her. And the little trick she discovered long ago of sounding out the words for her own ears to hear was not working this time—too many words she simply did not understand.

"Where did you get this, child?" Grandmother Linh looked up at Mai Tran who had been standing beside the old woman seated at the kitchen table. "This book speaks of events that have not yet happened."

"I know, Grandmother." Mai Tran had opened the large bound book to a page near the middle that displayed a map of North America—a map that appeared strangely unfamiliar to both of them. 'Texas' was the only word in the map caption that Mai Tran understood. Grandmother Linh closed the cover so that she could see the title of the book that her granddaughter had brought to her. It read *Lịch Sử Cận đạI 2001 - 2034*. To all appearances, this was a world history text book, printed in Vietnamese.

"Is this a make-believe book, Mai Tran?"

"No, Grandmother. This book was—will be—published twenty years from now."

"But—how? Where—?"

Mai Tran answered the question that her grandmother was attempting to ask. "I found it in the City last year—in a pawnshop. I understand much of what is written, but not this part." She turned back to the page with the map. "I don't understand what it is saying here, about the map. You see there are four countries shown here, not three."

Mai Tran was questioning the map of North America that showed Canada as expected, but with a large piece of the southern United States and a part of northeastern Mexico carved out of their respective countries, combined and together circumscribed with a new national border—a fourth large country on the North American continent. The old woman put her finger on a paragraph of text and read it silently to herself before offering a rough and halting English translation to her granddaughter.

Before leaving the apartment, Mai Tran asked her grandmother if she would keep the history book for her. "Can you hide it in a safe place for me, Ba Noi?"

The old woman hesitated for a moment before replying. "Yes, Mai Tran. I will keep it for you."

CHAPTER EIGHTEEN

DURING AN INTERVIEW with Governor Rick Perry in April 2009, Associated Press (AP) reporter Kelley Shannon commented to the Texas Governor, "Some have associated you with the idea of secession or sovereignty for your state."

The Governor responded, "I think there's a lot of different scenarios. Texas is a unique place. When we came in the Union in 1845, one of the issues was that we would be able to leave if we decided to do that. You know, my hope is that America—and Washington in particular—pays attention. We've got a great union. There is absolutely no reason to dissolve it. But if Washington continues to thumb their nose at the American people—you know—who knows what may come out of that? But Texas is a very unique place and we're a pretty independent lot to boot."

An immediate media frenzy ensued. How could a politician holding a position of responsibility as high as governor of the second largest state even consider that secession from the Union was a possible course of action? Supporters of the Governor suggested that the comments were intended to underscore the public frustration in some quarters with the path that the country had taken since the 2008 elections and that the notion of secession was not to be taken seriously.

After a few weeks, the controversy subsided but the story got new legs once Governor Perry announced his candidacy for the Republican nomination for President for the Election of 2012. While there was initial public excitement—both positive and negative—about the prospects of another Texas governor possibly winning the Presidency, the year prior to the election ended with no clear frontrunner from the Republican camp.

THE HISTORY OF TEXAS IS FILLED with many of the same elements that shaped the early history of the United States: European exploration, settlement, war and revolution. The region of the Southwest that included what is now the State of Texas was part of New Spain. And when Mexico won independence from Spain after years of conflict that ended with the signing of the Treaty of Córdoba in 1821, Texas was part of the new country. The new Mexican government encouraged immigration from the United States, and within a few years some thirty thousand Americans were living in Mexican Texas.

It wasn't long before the settlers in this northern state of Mexico felt as estranged from the seat of government in Mexico City as the Mexicans who had distanced themselves from their Spanish overlords only a few years earlier. In April 1830, the Mexican government issued a declaration that forbade further immigration from the U.S. and relations between the Texans and Mexico City degraded further.

The Texas Revolution began in 1835 and, to underscore his country's displeasure, President Santa

Anna personally led the contingent of the Mexican Army determined to quell the revolt.

On March 2, 1836, a Declaration of Independence was issued and the Republic of Texas was born. Only four days later, the Texas contingent of fighters who had been under siege at the Alamo for two weeks was overwhelmed by General Santa Anna's army. The Texan defeat at this outpost near San Antonio where no quarter was given by the Mexican Army led to the famous battle cry, "Remember the Alamo!"

Six weeks later, Santa Anna was defeated by Texas forces led by Sam Houston at the Battle of San Jacinto and independence for the new republic was won. Mexico has never recognized sovereignty of the Republic of Texas.

Two political factions quickly emerged in the new republic: one led by Sam Houston favored annexation as a state by the U.S., while the second faction was led by Mirabeau Lamar and called for continued independence and expansion of the western border of Texas to the Pacific Ocean. Lamar had come to Texas in 1835 after a varied career in Georgia as a state politician and publisher. But eventually, Houston's party prevailed and on December 29, 1845, Texas became the 28th state.

But statehood brought new hostilities. Mexico had long warned that any annexation of Texas by the United States would result in war and it began in earnest in 1846. The conflict continued for two years, but Mexican forces were no real match for the U.S. military and the Treaty of Guadalupe Hidalgo was signed in early 1848, ending the war. In addition to fixing the southern border of Texas at the Rio Grande,

Mexico ceded to the United States all land to the west, including what is now California, Nevada, Utah and most of Arizona.

CONTRARY TO MUCH POPULAR BELIEF, there was no specific provision within the first Texas State Constitution, ratified in 1845, allowing for the State to separate itself from the United States and become an independent nation as it had been during the preceding nine-year period. But by 1860, with the clouds of civil war fulminating on the horizon, the eventual secession of the southern states of the U.S. appeared unavoidable. In Texas, a voter referendum on secession in February 1861 resulted in a three-to-one margin in favor of leaving the Union. The outcome of the vote was not unexpected as the livelihood of a large percentage of the population depended upon cotton farming and the perceived necessity of maintaining the institution of slavery in the State.

The federal constitutionality of the referendum vote has long been debated. But it was the President and members of Congress of the northern states that ruled that neither secession nor a referendum on the subject was to be tolerated. Six southern states had left the union before the Texas secession vote.

The Civil War began on April 12, 1861, with the Confederate attack on Fort Sumter. By early June 1861, four other southern states joined the war effort on the side of the Confederacy.

When the war ended in 1865 and Texas was readmitted to the Union, the new Texas State Constitution—ratified in 1876—retained much of the language from the first State Constitution and included what many claim to be the legal justification for the modern Texas Secession Movement. Section 1 and Section 2 of the Texas State Constitution have been considered to be the pertinent constitutional bases for legal secession:

"SECTION 1. Texas is a free and independent State, subject only to the Constitution of the United States; and the maintenance of our free institutions and the perpetuity of the Union depend upon the preservation of the right of local self-government unimpaired to all the States.

SECTION 2. All political power is inherent in the people and all free governments are founded on their authority, and instituted for their benefit. The faith of the people of Texas stands pledged to the preservation of a republican form of government, and, subject to this limitation only, they have at all times the inalienable right to alter, reform or abolish their government in such manner as they may think expedient."

Proponents of the modern Texas Secession Movement are quick to emphasize that their state is subject to the Constitution of the United States and not to the U.S. Congress or the President of the United States.

CHAPTER NINETEEN

IT WAS TWO WEEKS since their last meeting at the Sands Hotel bar in Las Vegas. The Russian lit a cigarette and ordered another drink for Everett Adams. There had been no recurrence of Ev's migraine episode and he now considered it a freak, one-time event—certainly debilitating while it was happening, but hopefully unlikely to reoccur.

"And so, Everett, are preparations continuing as expected for the special exercise next Friday? I need to confirm with my people."

"Right on schedule. The only thing that could interfere at this point would be a major system failure or a freak summer storm."

"Excellent. But I must tell you something." The Russian hesitated before continuing. "We need you to make a change to your flight plan."

"What kind of change—and why?"

"The Nevada rendezvous point is not going to work; the assessment team needs more time with the aircraft."

"I don't understand." Ev made no attempt to conceal his displeasure with the Russian's surprise announcement. "Your people agreed on that location weeks ago."

"Ninety minutes is insufficient time for a thorough workup of the aircraft and any longer would risk detection. We have selected a more remote location."

"How remote?"

"Nuevo León."

"Mexico?" Ev was incredulous. "You've got to be kidding." The Russian was silent. Ev continued. "So I'm to report electrical problems with the aircraft on the way north to Fallon and then end up fifteen hundred miles away—in the opposite direction? Who will believe that story?"

"You won't need a story. My people will take good care of you; you won't be returning to the U.S. The Air Force will assume that you crashed somewhere in the Wassuk Mountains. It's a very remote area, unpopulated and with difficult terrain. They will search for a few weeks before giving up."

"Your people don't have enough money to convince me to abandon my life here. Where would I live? What would I do?"

"There are several charming resort towns along the Black Sea in the Ukraine and Bulgaria. We will find a nice one for you. Maybe in twenty years or so you can return to this country with a new identity. Meanwhile, you'll have two million dollars to provide some comfort for your loss of country."

THE EXERCISE HAD BEEN PLANNED for weeks. A single F-117A Nighthawk was to depart Groom Lake in time to arrive at the bombing range at the Naval Air Station in Fallon sometime between sunset on July 2nd and sunrise on July 3rd, the actual arrival time unknown to the air search radar operators. The crew in range operations at Fallon had set up the target—a surplus army truck illuminated by a helium-neon laser—earlier in the day. The mission would be deemed a success if the Nighthawk could penetrate the range undetected by radar and drop its payload of two Mk 84 two-thousand pound laser guided bombs on the target.

Ev Adams walked out of the BOQ at Groom Lake shortly before nine PM on July 2, 1982, and was driven to the hanger bay where the ground crew was preparing the Nighthawk for Ev's mission. He completed his pre-flight checks and was cleared for take-off by the control tower by quarter past ten.

The radar transponder in the Nighthawk was usually activated for routine flights so that military and civilian air controllers could "see" this otherwise undetectable aircraft. But for this test mission, the transponder was purposely switched off. Ev cleared the field and headed northwest toward Fallon, climbing to twenty-five thousand feet altitude.

The radar operators at Fallon had been peering into their CRT displays since sunset, scanning for any faint blip that might be the unknown aggressor aircraft that would be attempting to penetrate their "defenses" sometime that evening. But aside from a few false targets, they detected nothing. For the Mission Coordinator at Groom Lake, this was the happily expected result, but when Range Operations reported that the laser illuminated target truck was still sitting intact on the bombing range after eleven PM, Air Force officials knew that something was amiss. The Nighthawk should have completed the 220 mile run to

Fallon and dropped its bomb payload within forty-five minutes after takeoff. They attempted to raise Ev by radio to determine what had happened and to order him to activate the radar transponder. They got no response.

Less than half way to his presumed destination, Everett Adams had made a one-eighty degree turn and kept a steady eye on the altimeter as the Nighthawk climbed to fifty thousand feet. This altitude would keep him above the busy lanes of commercial aircraft transiting to and from the California coast that would otherwise cross his flight path. Maintaining a high altitude was vital from a safety standpoint. With no active transponder aboard the Nighthawk, radar on other aircraft would be unable to warn flight crews of a dangerous midair close encounter with Ev's plane. And the Nighthawk was equally blind as Ev dared not activate his own powerful air search radar lest the electromagnetic emissions—like electronic DNA—expose the unauthorized departure from his official flight plan and its attendant treachery.

While the Nighthawk's high ceiling would virtually guarantee no close encounters with commercial and general aviation aircraft, other military flights might still pose a problem. Consequently, Ev intended to pass safely north of Groom Lake and Nellis Air Force Base, then south over Lake Mead and into Arizona. After crossing the Arizona-New Mexico border, he would stay south of Albuquerque, passing over Roswell before turning further south and across West Texas to the Mexican border. Ev's final destination was to be an isolated airstrip—identified only by its coordinates—midway between Monterrey in the Mexican state of Nuevo León and Reynosa, directly across the border from McAllen, Texas.

The Nighthawk was to be met by a team of Soviet engineers and technicians who had arrived at the airstrip location at dusk, a few hours before Ev left Groom Lake. The military cargo plane, chosen because of its ability to land and take off from makeshift airstrips, had been diverted from Soviet air assets in Afghanistan and flown a few days earlier to Base Aérea San Antonio de los Baños, south of Havana. The flight to Nuevo León was completed successfully—avoiding detection by U.S. and Mexican air defenses through skillful piloting at extreme low-altitude over the Gulf of Mexico.

During the stopover in Cuba, the cargo bay had been filled with Royal Palm fronds and heavily-leafed cottonwood branches to serve as camouflage, to be strategically deployed after landing in Mexico in order to reduce the likelihood of a lucky detection of the aircraft and her crew by a U.S. spy satellite. It was a risky endeavor and attested to the importance that the Soviets placed on uncovering U.S. stealth technology secrets. Detection of a Soviet military aircraft uninvited on Mexican soil would have caused a serious international incident.

The Soviets waiting for Ev's Nighthawk at the airstrip began scanning the skies north of their location at dawn using high-powered binoculars. Immediately upon landing, the plan called for Ev to taxi to the open rear bay of the cargo plane where technicians would be waiting with portable diamond blade industrial saws. The bay of the aircraft was not wide enough to receive a completely intact Nighthawk, so the fuselage and severed wings were to be loaded separately.

But by 8 AM, Everett Adams was nearly three hours overdue. In the opinion of the Soviet mission commander, the American had either crashed, or become lost, or had changed his mind about defecting and turning his aircraft over to America's archenemy.

The commander passed the word that the team was to stand down, and if the Nighthawk didn't show up within the next hour, the crew was to pack up and then get some rest prior to departure later in the day. Somebody—maybe several people—would pay for the failure of this critical Soviet mission. It was the mission commander's hope that he could avoid getting on the list of the blamed that would soon be compiled in some deep recess of the Kremlin.

The cargo plane would leave from the airstrip the same way it arrived—at dusk, hugging the terrain and skimming above the surface of the Gulf until over international waters. The mission crew would make a refueling stop in Cuba and another in Egypt before arriving at Levashovo Airbase, near Leningrad, with an empty cargo bay.

CHAPTER TWENTY

AT ELEVEN PM, instead of having just dropped the payload of the two laser-guided bombs on the truck target in Fallon, Everett Adams' Nighthawk was more than three hundred miles away, fifty thousand feet above U.S Route 93 northeast of his Groom Lake home base, and now there was no turning back. Up to that point he could have returned to base, justifying his decision to abort the bombing run by fabricating a report of intermittent radio and engine problems, but now he was committed to completing the alternate mission that he and the Russian had agreed upon.

On approach to Lake Mead, he reduced his elevation to 2,200 feet—about one thousand feet above the surface—and released his bomb payload, unarmed, into the center of the lake before commencing the climb back to the former high altitude. This was a precaution: the landing at the airstrip in Mexico would be tricky enough even without the safety factor and weight reduction afforded by jettisoning the bombs and arriving at the rendezvous point with a nearly empty fuel load, drained after the long flight.

For Ev, everything was proceeding according to plan. Weather conditions were perfect, and the Nighthawk was performing beautifully, with engine temperature and fuel consumption within specified limits. But shortly after crossing into Chaves County, New Mexico, the mission began to unravel. It started with some moderate buffeting of the airframe that seemed to start coincidentally as the blackness of the night was suddenly overcome by a diffuse white light coming from no specific direction. "What the hell?" Ev asked himself. "It's too early to be sunlight."

The needles on the gauges in his instrument cluster began to jump. The buffeting increased and the white light penetrating the cockpit was now nearly blinding. Ev had never experienced anything like this before. All hope of restoring normal operation vanished when both turbofan engines suddenly shut down and the Nighthawk began to tumble. Without engine power, the built-in stability recovery system was useless and Everett Adams now knew that he had no other option but to eject from his aircraft.

The Nighthawk was losing altitude rapidly, yet Ev's altimeter was not changing—stuck at 45,000 feet—and he could only guess at his current true altitude and rate of descent. From his prior training he understood that surviving an ejection at high altitude could not be guaranteed. But after delaying only about twenty seconds, the increasingly violent tumbling of the Nighthawk was threatening a loss of consciousness and Ev pulled the ejection seat handle.

First a loud bang, then a rush of wind against his flight suit, and finally a jerk as the canopy of his parachute filled with air. He was once again enveloped in near darkness and now, in the quiet of his descent, he began to consider for the first time what horrific consequences might be ultimately awaiting him below, in the desert just outside Roswell, New Mexico.

CHAPTER TWENTY-ONE

DR. DANFORTH WAS SKEPTICAL of the results of several mass spectrometer analysis reports of the silicon crystal material that he and his Bell Labs research team had been tasked to assess. He spoke to the technician who had been performing the mass spectrometer tests on a lab bench nearby.

"These all look like copies of the very same test."

"I don't know what to tell you, Doctor Danforth. All of the samples you gave me tested out with exactly the same fraction of the impurity, about one part in ten thousand."

"And no other trace elements? Just essentially pure silicon with this same proportion of arsenic?"

"Yes, sir."

"Then I think we can fairly well assume that the arsenic is not an impurity, but was purposely added to the pure silicon, and probably in a specified proportion." Danforth continued, "We need to get a closer look inside this material."

Bell Labs had only one electron microscope and a team of specialized technicians was needed to keep it running at top performance. It would be two days before Danforth could get a look inside the crystal lattice structure of his silicon-arsenic material.

Only with the invention of the electron microscope by German engineers in the 1930s was this even possible. No microscope can resolve any detail finer than the wavelength of the light used to create the image. This limits the useful magnification of an optical microscope to about 1300x. But the equivalent wavelength of an electron is far smaller and an electron microscope can resolve detail a thousand times smaller than the best optical microscopes. Magnifications of one million times or more are commonly observed.

At first glance, the black-and-white prints of the images of the silicon material appeared to show only repetitive, uniform crystalline structure that one would expect from pure silicon. However, a closer examination revealed occasional slight irregularity in the structure.

"See that!" Dr. Danforth was excited. "There—and there. Those are arsenic atoms displacing some of the silicon in the lattice. . . ." He paused. "And I think I understand why!" He rushed to the blackboard in the room and began to quickly erase the equations that someone had previously scrawled—he needed to free up some drawing space on the board. Danforth stopped suddenly, reminding himself that this wasn't his blackboard, nor even his office. "I'm sorry." Still holding the felt eraser, he turned to the other scientists and technicians in the room.

The head of the microscopy lab replied, "Don't apologize, Doctor Danforth. Please continue. We're all interested."

Danforth turned back to the board and drew a grid of squares in white chalk. "This represents our silicon crystal lattice." Then he picked up the yellow chalk and drew a few random squares over the white ones. "And these are arsenic atoms which have displaced some of the silicon atoms. Arsenic has five valence electrons, but only four of them are shared with their nearest silicon atom neighbors, maintaining the lattice structure. The fifth electron is unbound." He waited for a response from the onlookers. "Don't you see? If an electric field is present, these free electrons will move through the lattice like shit through a Christmas goose! With a few arsenic atoms diffused into otherwise pure silicon, this non-conductor can now carry a current like a metal, but that can be controlled with an electric field."

One of the scientists in the room understood the implication of this finding. "So a device could be designed using this stuff that could replace a vacuum tube?"

"Exactly," added Danforth, "for amplification or in switching applications."

One of the technicians expressed his thoughts on this discovery aloud. "With scientists like the ones that invented this, I keep wondering how the German's lost the war." Others in the room murmured in agreement.

Danforth countered. "I don't know about that. I've read a lot of the translated research documents that the Army captured—including papers by Tessla before he died and some from the Nazi labs in Unter-Turkheim near Stuttgart. I saw nothing like this in those papers. Not from this earth, in my humble opinion."

"HOW CAN I HELP YOU, GEORGE?" George Cramer was a Junior Physicist, working for Dr. Danforth at Bell Labs. He had been present in the microscopy laboratory just an hour earlier when Danforth gave his impromptu dissertation. Dr. Cramer had come to see the Senior Physicist in his private office. He turned to close the office door before answering.

"I need to ask you some questions, if that's OK."

"Shoot!"

"Do you know Harold Edgerton?"

"Yes. I met him at M.I.T. years ago—a brilliant engineer, in my opinion."

"Have you seen him since then?"

"In '44, I think it was—at Alamogordo. I was called in to do some consulting work for the Manhattan Project. Can't go into any detail, of course, it's still Top Secret stuff."

"Did you know that he's about to open a new startup engineering business with a couple of partners, Ken Germehausen and Herb Grier?"

"I've heard the rumors. Germehausen was a graduate student, working under Edgerton at M.I.T. I believe they're going to call the firm 'Edgerton, Germehausen & Grier'—original name, don't you think?" Danforth was smirking. "But what's this all about, George? Are you thinking about going to work for them? Have they approached you?"

"No, nothing like that." Dr. Cramer paused before continuing. "The electronic devices that were sent to us from Wright-Patterson—the ones we believe came from the crash site in New Mexico—the ones we've been studying for the last few months. . . ."

"Yes. What about them, George?"

"There have been no manufacturer's markings on any of the parts I've examined—nothing in English or German and no alien hieroglyphics. No markings whatsoever until I opened the last box in the shipment two days ago."

George Cramer reached into the pocket of his white lab coat and threw a handful of electronic chips on to the surface of the desk where Danforth was seated. They were small black components—different sizes—up to maybe two inches long and a half-inch wide with a row of gold-colored metal contacts running along both long edges. Danforth picked up one of pieces and examined it closely. "I pulled these off of several unmarked circuit boards that were in that box," added Dr. Cramer.

Danforth examined a second, then a third piece. The black surface of each had identical markings. "This looks like silk screen printing. Who—or what—is 'EG&G Reticon'?"

"Who else could it be—but Edgerton, Germehausen & Grier?"

CHAPTER TWENTY-TWO

AS EVERETT ADAMS DESCENDED in near darkness toward the New Mexico desert floor his mind was racing. The apparent mechanical or electronic failure of the Nighthawk—he was unsure which—couldn't have come at a worse time. How could he possibly explain to Air Force investigators why his aircraft was two states—a thousand miles—away from his official mission destination?

Collecting his thoughts as his feet touched down near the top of a small rise, Ev reasoned that his best chance of avoiding eventual prosecution and imprisonment over this affair required that he distance himself as far as possible from the crash location of the Nighthawk. Once the wreckage was found and identified he would immediately become the subject of a possible espionage investigation and a manhunt would invariably be initiated.

Where could he go? Perhaps slipping south across the Mexican border would be his best option. Because it was still pre-dawn and the region seemed only sparsely populated, there was some chance that the wreckage might lie undetected for days or weeks or more. But he couldn't count on that favorable eventuality.

He had witnessed the ground impact of his out-of-control aircraft while he was still a thousand feet or more above the ground. The Nighthawk had augured into the New Mexico desert some few miles—he guessed—to the northwest of his location. The impact was pretty loud, but fortunately for Ev, flames from the crash explosion quickly extinguished themselves.

Just before his aircraft had started to malfunction, the Nighthawk navigation screen indicated the nearest town was Roswell, New Mexico. He could see some dim lights—from the town, he supposed—several miles away to the southeast and after burying his helmet, parachute and jacket of his flight suit under some rocks, he set off in that direction.

THE SCATTERED LIGHTS IN THE TOWN were slowly extinguished as the pre-dawn eastern sky began to brighten. It was going to be a hot day, and Ev was thankful when the driver of the old Ford truck coming up behind him on the dirt road slowed down to offer a ride.

"It's quite a few miles into town. Why don't you hop in? I'm going that way."

Ev didn't hesitate. He opened the passenger door and jumped in. "Thanks for stopping. It's pretty desolate out here." Ev extended his hand to the driver, a young man that Ev judged to be in his mid twenties. "I'm Everett—uh—Everett Brady. What's your name?" Ev had almost given his full real name. He would have to be more careful in the future.

"George—," replied the driver. "—George Landry. You're not from around here, are you?"

"No—just passing through. I broke down a few miles back."

"You know, I'm a pretty good mechanic," offered the driver. "I've got some time. We could go back and see if I can get you started."

Ev had to think quickly and come up with a good reason not to accept the young man's help. "Thanks for the offer, but I think I may have blown the engine—maybe ran it out of oil."

"Then I'll take you to a garage. You can hire a tow truck." Ev nodded in approval. The driver kept his truck in second gear so it was hard to hear over the whine of the transmission. George had to keep his speed below twenty miles an hour or the truck would buck violently due to the washboard condition of the road.

"You've got a pretty nice truck here, George. Is it a '48 model?" Ev was impressed as the old truck looked as if it had been restored to nearly mint condition.

"No," replied George, "it's a '47. The new model won't be out for a few more months." Ev didn't quite understand George's answer, but passed it off. George continued, "This one was pretty hard to find. Had to go clear to Lubbock and it cost me fifteen hundred cash."

"At that price, I'd say you stole it," offered Ev.

Starting about a mile from town the road surface turned to asphalt and George was able to speed up to the forty mile per hour posted limit. And for the first time this morning they encountered some oncoming traffic. Ev thought it curious that the cars passing in the opposite direction on West Pine Lodge Road were all pretty old. When George turned on to Second Street, Ev couldn't help but notice that none of the cars parked along both sides of the street were any newer than George's old truck and that most of the newer models seemed to be in remarkably good condition.

"So—" offered Ev, "there must me some antique car show in town today?"

"Not that I know of." George didn't understand why Ev had made the comment. But when they came up upon the local Chevrolet dealership, Ev asked George to pull over and stop.

"I think I'll get out here. I'd like to check out that Chevy convertible in the showroom."

"Sure thing, Everett. Might be a good move to get a new car if you really blew the engine on your old one. It's an expensive repair."

Everett Adams stepped down from the truck, then turned and leaned through the open passenger window, facing the driver. "Thanks very much, George, for the lift. I really appreciate it."

"Good luck to you, Everett."

THE CAR IN THE SHOWROOM was dark blue with a cream colored interior and fat white wall tires. In all respects it looked brand new, but what caused Ev's double-take was the hand-written white cardboard sign leaning against the windshield:

1947 CHEVROLET CONVERTIBLE
6 CYLINDER
$1,628
FINANCING AVAILABLE

"It's a real beauty, don't you think?" The salesman wore a brown tweed suit and red tie. He waited for some response from Ev, but there was none. "Oh—I know what you're thinking. A little pricey, huh? Well the price is firm. You won't find another one like it within five hundred miles, but I could make you a good deal on one of these sedans—they're used, but very few miles on 'em. They're both '46 models." Ev turned his eye to the Chevy sedans—one grey and one black—toward the back of the showroom. "They both have the same six cylinder, ninety horsepower engine as that new convertible."

Ev Adams' head was spinning. "What the hell is going on here?" he thought to himself and then asked the salesman, "Could I get some water? And I need to sit for a minute."

"Sure thing. Come on over to my desk. I'll get some water for you." The salesman led Ev past the two used sedans to one of two wooden chairs in front of his sales desk against the back wall of the showroom, then proceeded to the water bubbler and filled a cone-shaped paper cup from the spigot. Returning to his desk, he passed the cup to Ev and sat down. "If you don't mind me saying, you look like you've been up all night."

"That's about right." Ev realized that he had become dehydrated and wasn't feeling well. He drained the cup. "Thanks for the water. Could I have another?" The salesman nodded and took Ev's cup back to bubbler and filled it. Ev knew something wasn't quite right about the showroom and especially the price of that like-new Chevy convertible. The décor reminded him of what one might see in an old black-and-white film from the 1940s or early 50s: the plain linoleum flooring, the green-glass shade of the lamp on the salesman's desk, an old black telephone and vintage Marchant mechanical calculator on a nearby table—all old stuff but seemingly little worn; in an as-new condition. And Ev knew that a well-restored Chevrolet convertible from the late forties would easily bring five or ten times the posted price of this one and far more if you could even find one anywhere in the same pristine condition. After downing the second cup of water and glancing down at the newspaper on the salesman's desk, he was startled as he read to himself from his upside-down view of the headline:

WAR DEPT CHIEF SAYS PACIFIC
A-TESTS TO RESUME NEXT YEAR

War Department? Ev knew that the Department of Defense was no longer referred to as the 'War Department' after 1947, and there had been no nuclear weapons tests conducted in the Pacific since the Christmas Island testing in 1962. His head started spinning again. "Could I see your newspaper?" Ev asked the salesman.

"No problem. Here ya' go. . . ." The salesman passed the paper to Ev, who immediately focused on the publication date. The paper in Everett Adam's hands was the *Roswell Daily Record* of Tuesday, July 1, 1947.

"I gotta go." Ev quickly rose from his chair and made a beeline for the exit on the street side of the showroom.

The salesman called out to him, "I know you want this car. Make me an offer!" Ev acknowledged the salesman's proposal with only a raised hand. He didn't even turn around, and after a few seconds he was pacing rapidly down the sidewalk along Second Street.

"What's happening here?" Ev thought to himself. "Where the hell am I?" Now the anachronisms to his 1982 frame of reference were bombarding him: The Shell gasoline station across the street prominently displayed a price placard proclaiming "regular" gas for 18.9 cents per gallon. At the gas pumps, a station attendant was serving his customer by actually filling the gas tank and checking the oil level while the customer remained in the driver's seat of his car. And walking past the mom-and-pop grocery store he saw a carefully laid out stack of Jonathan apples in one storefront window offered at five cents each and navel oranges in a second window at nineteen cents a pound.

He was tired and stressed out and had to think. Up ahead near the end of the block above the sidewalk he could see the large painted sign of the Roswell Hotel. The hotel was a three-story brick structure built out to the edge of the sidewalk. Ev entered the lobby and stepped to the registration counter.

"Can I help you?"

"Yes, I need a room for a couple of nights."

"OK, but check-in time isn't until one PM."

"That's fine—I'll pay for the extra day. I'm very tired and need to get into the room right now."

"Certainly, sir. The room is four-twenty-five per day; five dollars with a private bath, payable in advance. Please sign the guest register." The clerk turned the book for Ev to sign and handed him a pen. "You have no luggage?"

"No. It's in my car that broke down outside of town. I'll get it later." Ev signed in as Everett Brady and opened his wallet—hesitating for a moment. Would the clerk accept his 1982 money or would it look odd and raise suspicion? He didn't know if the bill designs had changed since 1947. Ev had a dozen hundreds and a few twenties. If you were a gambler, you always carried a lot of cash. He handed the clerk a twenty. "I'll need a room with a bath." Ev was relieved to see that the clerk took no particular notice of the bill.

"We're pretty empty so far this week, so you have your choice of floors: first, second or third."

"First floor, please," replied Ev. The clerk turned to the wall behind him and pulled the key marked '1D' from its hook. He scrawled out a receipt and handed it to Ev along with a ten dollar bill and a pair of singles as change.

"I gave you a little discount for the late check-in." The clerk sounded almost apologetic. "Check out time is noon tomorrow, unless you have a change of plans. Your room is down the hall, on the right."

Ev nodded in acknowledgement and headed toward the hallway. There was a small seating area in the lobby and Ev passed a magazine rack. "Do you mind if I borrow a couple of these? I'll return them in the morning."

"Not a problem, Mr. Brady. Have a good rest." Ev picked up a copy of *Time Magazine* and the local newspaper—it was same edition that he saw at the Chevy dealership. Inside his room Ev sat on the double bed—a little lumpy, he thought—and took off his boots. He leaned back on a pillow and closed his eyes. In less than five minutes Everett Adams was sound asleep.

CHAPTER TWENTY-THREE

THE REPORT OF THE MISSING Nighthawk had reached the Air Staff and the Office of the Secretary of the Air Force in the Pentagon by 9 AM. The Secretary had been briefed via secure telephone and was assured that a maximum effort was already underway to locate the downed aircraft, hopefully with both pilot and airplane reasonably intact. The fact that it was down was self-evident. The question was where. Obviously, there was no radar track due to the very nature of the mission and the stealth characteristics of the missing aircraft.

Search and Rescue planners laid out a fan-shaped search area running from Groom Lake northwest to a point beyond Lake Tahoe on one side and Mt. Moses on the other. Although Everett Adams was a skilled test pilot it was also possible that he had flown beyond the intended strike point at NAS Fallon. For this reason, the initial search area—covering some twenty-five thousand square miles—would extend as far north as Pyramid Lake. If necessary, it would be extended even further.

Although neither Fallon nor Groom Lake had air assets designed specifically for Search and Rescue, conventional aircraft had been dispatched from both locations shortly after daybreak due to the urgency of the situation.

Favorable weather conditions facilitated the early search efforts. By mid-afternoon, officers and staff from the Aerospace Rescue and Recovery Service had arrived at Fallon. Three Sikorsky Seaguard helicopters were sent from Whidbey Island Naval Air Station and a pair of Lockheed HC-130H Hercules search aircraft from McChord Field in Washington State. Counting all of the support staff, the search team quickly grew to over 200 military and civilian personnel.

The visible high level of military air activity in the Nevada skies began to attract attention from news agencies and a press release was issued. Everett Adams was named as the civilian test pilot whose Lockheed-instrumented Gates Learjet—purposely misidentified—disappeared between Groom Lake and NAS Fallon while on a routine test flight. The pilot's aunt, Betty Anderson, was listed as his next-of-kin and was notified at her home in Texas that the young man was missing.

HOPE FOR AN EARLY and successful outcome for the search effort began to fade by the fifth full day after Everett Adams began his mission. The Distress Radio Beacon aboard the aircraft would have been activated automatically in the event of a major impact or could be activated manually by the pilot if he were alive and conscious after a crash. No beacon signal was detected and battery power for the device would have been exhausted after the third day. The Search and Rescue effort was redesignated as one of Search and Recovery.

The loss of one Nighthawk airplane and test pilot would be a significant but recoverable setback for the Air Force program, but what worried officials in the highest level A-Ring offices of the Pentagon was the possibility that the incident would lead to public revelation of the very existence of the super-secret stealth airplane. In fact, it would be nearly ten years later—in 1991—before existence of the F117A Nighthawk was revealed to the world with its first wartime deployment during Operation Desert Storm.

After two weeks of receiving nothing but negative reports, the Secretary of the Air Force scheduled a personal visit to NAS Fallon to get a firsthand look and review of the search effort. The participants at the briefing included a dozen of the most senior members of the search team.

Although short on results, the presentation underscored the thoroughness of the search effort. One of the slides presented by Captain Zachary Brown, Commanding Officer at Fallon, contained the following information:

PREVIOUSLY UNKNOWN CRASH SITES
DISCOVERED AS A RESULT OF
CURRENT SEARCH EFFORT

LOCKHEED P-38 LIGHTNING, LOST JANUARY 1942, DISCOVERED ON WEST FACE OF MOUNT TOBIN AT 8,000 FT LEVEL

REPUBLIC P-47 THUNDERBOLT, LOSS DATE UNKNOWN, DISCOVERED IN WILDERNESS AREA 10 MILES NORTHEAST OF VIRGINIA CITY

PIPER CHEROKEE, LOST NOVEMBER 1980, DISCOVERED ON SOUTH EAST FACE OF MOUNT GRANT AT 10,000 FT LEVEL

GULFSTREAM IIB, LOST OCTOBER 1978, DISCOVERED ON SOUTH FACE OF MOUNT GRANT AT 9,000 FT LEVEL

McDONNELL DOUGLAS F-15 EAGLE, LOST FEBRUARY 1977, DISCOVERED SOUTH OF LAHONTAN STATE RECREATION AREA

UH60A BLACKHAWK HELICOPTER, LOST DECEMBER 1975, DISCOVERED IN EAST FOOTHILS OF JOBS PEAK

Captain Brown noted that the collateral discovery of these previously unknown crash sites might at least bring some closure to the families of the lost civilian pilots and passengers and the military personnel.

For his closing comments, the Commanding Officer at Fallon asked the A/V operator to redisplay an earlier slide showing the map of Nevada with an overlay grid of the search area.

“As of today we have completed a thorough search of over ninety percent of the initial grid area. By the end of the week, it will be 100 percent complete with the exception of some possible water locations. If Everett Adams and his aircraft remain undiscovered by this weekend, the search will be extended north to the Nevada-Washington state line."

The Captain pointed at the border location on the map and continued, "and we will initiate a search in the waters of these four lakes," he said, pointing at each as he enumerated them. "Walker Lake, Carson Lake, Lake Tahoe and Pyramid Lake." Now grasping both ends of the pointer staff in his hands and holding it in front of him, the Captain turned to the attendees. "This concludes my prepared remarks. Are there any questions?"

"I have one, Zack." The question came from Secretary Orr. "Isn't searching Tahoe going to present a problem? It's a big lake and—as I understand—pretty deep."

"You are correct, Mr. Secretary. Lake Tahoe is 1,600 feet at its deepest point. We have located a small ocean submersible in the San Diego area. It's in transit as we speak and should arrive in South Lake Tahoe with its commercial crew sometime tomorrow. There are some security clearance issues to be ironed out, but we don't anticipate major problems. We believe we can cover the other three lakes with surface vessels and deploy Navy divers if necessary." With the briefing completed, Secretary Orr stepped to the podium to address the briefing participants.

"I want to express my sincere thanks to the Commanding Officers of both Groom Lake and NAS Fallon for not only their informative presentations today, but also for their untiring and dedicated efforts over the last two weeks in leading the search for our missing aviator and aircraft. I further extend my thanks to the entire search team. Clearly, you people know how to find missing airplanes. You need to find just one more."

The Secretary's last remark produced a ripple of tittering laughter from some members of the seated audience. Secretary Orr continued, "I received a call from Secretary Weinberger yesterday before leaving Washington. He assured me that he understands the difficulty of this effort—as does President Reagan—but it is essential that we continue the search to a successful conclusion. Thank you for your continuing efforts and dedication, and I look forward to receiving some positive reports."

CHAPTER TWENTY-FOUR

LONG BEFORE THE FIRST EUROPEANS arrived in what is now New Mexico, the land was inhabited by the indigenous people from several tribes, notably the Apache, Pueblo and Navajo. Life for these Native Americans was irreversibly altered beginning with the arrival of an expedition from Mexico led by Francisco Vásquez de Coronado in 1541. Coronado was in search of the elusive Seven Golden Cities of Cibola, a place described by to him by another explorer, Cabeza de Vaca. De Vaca had never actually seen the seven cities. His description was based on rumors and legends of the Native Americans.

Neither Coronado, nor anyone else, was able to find the Seven Golden Cities, but the settlers that followed did find a land that promised great potential, well-suited for raising cattle and sheep and fertile soil for agriculture. But it was not an easy life for the early settlers and even less so for the indigenous people who were exploited—first by the Spaniards, then the Mexican governors.

By the time that American settlers began to arrive after the war and treaty with Mexico, the tribes in the region understood that an uneasy peace, punctuated by periods of intense conflict, was the best they could hope for as long as they dared to live freely in the land of their ancestors.

THE TOWN OF ROSWELL was named by Van Smith in honor of his father, Roswell Smith, a lawyer from Indiana. Van Smith came to the Roswell area from Omaha. Sources disagree as to his profession. He was a businessman—or possibly a gambler. He and his partner built two adobe structures in 1869 that housed a general store and post office.

Cattle and sheep ranches dotted the surrounding countryside, thanks to the presence of water springs in the area. The largest cattle ranch in the region was owned by John Chisum. His ranch, located only five miles from Roswell, marked the beginning of the "Chisum Trail" to Las Cruces where cattle were loaded on rail cars destined for northern and eastern markets. The ranches were often targets of Apache raiding parties. Skirmishes between white ranchers and the Apaches continued until the late 1880s.

The town grew slowly until the accidental 1890 discovery of a massive aquifer capable of supplying the water needs of a much larger city. Roswell was incorporated in 1891 and acquired rail service in 1893. In 1912, New Mexico became the 47th state in the Union.

IMPORTANT SCIENTIFIC and military activity began in Roswell in the 1930s. Dr. Robert Goddard, considered by most to be the father of modern rocketry, chose the Roswell area for developing and testing his liquid fuel rockets. Ironically, the Nazi government in Germany proved to be far more interested in Goddard's published research than the U.S. War Department. Liquid fuels—alcohol/water and liquid oxygen—propelled the German V-2s that rained down on London and Antwerp during the last year of the war in Europe. These ballistic missiles also applied Goddard's work on gyroscopic stabilization to improve performance. Robert Goddard was a patriot and worked for the U.S. Navy during World War Two.

A military flying school was established in Roswell by the U.S. Army in 1941 after acquiring land from a local rancher, David Chesser. The school was activated in September, just prior to America entering the War. In 1942 the base became known as Roswell Army Air Field. The 509th Bomb Group, famous for B-29 Superfortress bombing raids on Japan from the airbase on the Pacific island of Tinian, relocated to Roswell Army Air Field in November 1945.

DOCTOR THOMAS STARK, the President and founder of Wormstone Engineering signed the government contract to provide support services at Roswell Army Air Field on March 31, 1944. Construction of the firm's facility on Y.O. Road in Roswell commenced the next month and was completed in 45 days.

There were several contractors in direct support of the war effort for the Army in Roswell. For most of these companies, the end of the war meant termination of their contracts. But the Army had a continuing requirement for the basic services provided by Wormstone Engineering, including the repair and refurbishment of electronic modules and courier services.

Wormstone management was pleased when the government chose to exercise the contract options for continuing the level of effort for at least another three years and the original contract was renewed several more times after that. While many of her neighboring firms had closed down, leaving vacant buildings, there was plenty of activity at the Wormstone facility in July 1947, on Y.O. Road.

CHAPTER TWENTY-FIVE

AFTER LEARNING from his Soviet handlers that the mission to snatch the Nighthawk aircraft had failed, Leo the Russian spent the next several weekends cruising the casinos that his poker partners, Everett Adams and Anthony Costello, had been frequenting earlier in the year. The whole affair had been an embarrassment to Leo and his KGB superiors, and if he ever found Everett Adams, he wasn't certain exactly how seriously he would express his displeasure. To the Russian, it was fairly obvious that Adams had a change of heart at the last minute and decided against following through with the conspiracy plan.

It was not until the first Friday evening in September that the Russian—seated at the bar near the entrance to the Sands Hotel—observed Anthony Costello checking in, accompanied by a young woman. There was no sign of Ev Adams. He decided he would wait until Costello had settled into his room and returned to the casino floor before approaching him and inquiring concerning the whereabouts of Everett Adams.

"I'M SORRY, LEO. IF I HAD KNOWN how to get in touch with you, I would have told you about Ev. He was on a nighttime test flight more than a month ago and he never returned. Must have crashed somewhere in the mountains, but they haven't been able to find him or the plane. They are still searching."

How persistent these Americans are, Leo thought to himself. "I'm so sorry to hear this news." The Russian didn't know how to process this revelation. Was it true? Or was Costello simply baiting him? Ev Adams may have spilled the plot to Air Force authorities who were waiting at this moment to arrest him.

The Russian reflexively looked about for possible undercover agents among the hotel patrons, but saw no one that looked likely. Finally, he reasoned to himself that if the plot were known, the authorities would have found and arrested him weeks ago. So perhaps it was true that Ev had crashed and was killed.

The airplane wreckage may have remained undiscovered because the Air Force would have little reason to search anywhere except along the mission flight plan between Groom Lake and Fallon. And if Ev was committed to the conspiracy, he could have crashed anywhere between Southern Nevada and Northern Mexico. "If you learn anything further about Everett, please let me know." Leo handed a business card to Anthony Costello.

CHAPTER TWENTY-SIX

EVERETT ADAMS WOKE UP after six hours of restless sleep. He had finally accepted the apparent fact that his temporal frame of reference had been mysteriously shifted by thirty-five years. And he was thankful for it, considering the alternative of hiding out indefinitely to avoid almost certain prosecution and imprisonment. Attempting to disclose military secrets that would compromise the security of the country was a serious crime, even if the attempt proved unsuccessful.

But all that was part of a previous life. He was now twenty-seven year old Everett Brady and he needed to create a new identity for himself. Ev opened his wallet and removed his Nevada driver's license and Lockheed Employee ID. These pieces of paper and plastic represented the only evidence that could point to his true past. He felt some small measure of regret as he set the documents afire and watched as the ashes of his former life fell into the commode and were flushed away.

Ev's parents had both passed away when he was very young and Ev was raised by an Aunt whose husband was a Navy pilot. While growing up in Caldwell, Texas, his Aunt often talked about her husband, George Anderson, the step-father that Ev never knew. George Anderson was killed in the Pacific during World War II.

One of young Everett's favorite stories—which he begged his Aunt to repeat again and again—was how his step-father had trouble persuading the Army recruiter in Austin to allow him to enlist. The young man had a youthful face for his age and the recruiter didn't believe his explanation for why he could not produce a birth certificate to prove he was old enough to enlist. The Caldwell County Courthouse in Lockhart burned down in 1928 and all the birth, death and real estate title records were lost.

Ev figured that he could come up with no better explanation for why there was no record of Everett Brady's birth in Caldwell in—say—1923. Ev looked in the mirror and thought, "I can pass for a twenty-four year old."

Ev picked up the copy of the 30 June 1947 issue of *Time Magazine* that he had borrowed from the hotel lobby. He flipped through the pages, hoping to get a sense of the times that were now a part of his life. In the "milestones" section, he read of the marriage in Akron, Ohio, of William Clay Ford and Martha Firestone, grandchildren of the two late auto industry moguls, Henry Ford and Harvey Firestone.

The magazine cover story featured Mohandas Kamarchand Gandhi. This article described the high hopes that Gandhi had for India as it prepared for independence from Great Britain and the elevated level of anxiety in the country about conflicting Moslem and Hindu interests as the British were about to make a fast exit from the region.

Another article that Ev found interesting described the growing militarism in Korea—especially in the northern part of the country—foreshadowing the Korean War that he knew would break out in another three years.

Ev was tired. It had been a long day and the few hours of sleep he had were far from restful. He dozed off again after a half-hour of reading.

TWO EGGS, BACON, HASH BROWNS, toast and coffee for just seventy-five cents was the breakfast special scribbled on the blackboard on the wall of the Sunshine Coffee Shop next to the hotel. Ev had awakened early and was starved. By the time he had finished breakfast and was on his third cup of coffee, the establishment had begun to fill up with the workweek morning regulars.

Ev had brought the newspaper from the hotel and was perusing the classified ads. He needed to find three things soon: a job, a reliable but inexpensive vehicle and a place to live.

CHAPTER TWENTY-SEVEN

IT WAS 9AM on the morning after their meeting with Marjorie Hedrick when Amanda Marshall and Roger Atwood drove out of the hotel parking lot on North Main Street in the rented Jeep. After fifteen minutes, Roger turned on to Y.O. Road and slowed down, again checking out the few open and many shuttered businesses along the route they had traveled previously. Roger proceeded past the vacant Wormstone Engineering building and continued for a few hundred feet before turning around.

Now confident that they hadn't been followed and after concluding that there were no suspicious characters in the vicinity, Roger pulled into the parking lot, drove past the tarp-shrouded pickup truck that was still there after their previous visit and parked. Their objective was the structure next to the building they had searched just two days before. Marjorie Hedrick had told them that the Army had commandeered the former auto repair business and used it to reconstruct the wreckage from the 1947 Roswell crash.

"Do you think that maybe we should go back into the Wormstone main building, Roger? Maybe we missed something."

"No, but—" Roger pulled on the handle of the door that they had entered two days earlier and found that it wouldn't open. "—but we left this door unlocked. Someone has been here since our last visit." As they walked past the corner of the building and headed in the direction of the adjacent structure, Roger added, "Let's see if there is anything interesting next door."

The structure—the converted auto repair business—appeared to have been abandoned for years, maybe for decades. As they walked the perimeter of the building, Roger tried both the front and side entry doors as well as each of the three roll-up bay doors, but all were locked down.

The Jalousie windows—the type with frameless narrow overlapping panes of plate glass arranged horizontally—were obscured with a heavy coat of paint, the same paint that covered the entire concrete block structure of the building. Even the large plate glass window near the front entrance had been similarly painted over. "Clearly," offered Amanda, "someone has made a serious effort here to keep anyone from looking in."

Back at the rear of the building and hidden from view from the street, Roger began to scrape away the heavy coat of paint covering one of the plate glass window panes using the ignition key from the Jeep. "Here, Roger. Use this." Amanda offered him a short-bladed jack knife that she had dug up from the bottom of her purse.

"So when did you start carrying a weapon?" Roger quipped. It took only a few minutes for him to cleanly scrape away all of the paint from a six-inch wide section on one of the narrow panes. Then he peered in.

The interior of the building was surprisingly well lit, with illumination coming from several overhead skylights. Roger could see a single large, dusty canvas tarpaulin completely covering something. That something could have been one very large object or many smaller ones; it was impossible to tell which. Whatever was under that tarp occupied much of the interior floor space of the building, spanning all three of the hydraulic lifts that had been originally used to service customer vehicles. There was a small table with three or four chairs near the corner of the building to his left.

"Take a look." Roger stepped aside, motioning for Amanda to take a turn at the cleared window pane.

Amanda took a full minute to scan the entire building interior, left to right and top to bottom, before commenting. "Maybe we found it. Maybe under that tarp is the wreckage of the craft that Dieter Hedrick recovered in the desert. You think it could be, after all these years?"

"Why don't we all go inside and find out?" The booming voice from behind Roger and Amanda startled them, and they turned to see who it was that had apparently been watching and eavesdropping on their conversation. Amanda recognized his face.

"Doctor Tushenkov! What a surprise to see you here in New Mexico—especially in Roswell. When we spoke last, you told me that you had closed your Roswell facility years ago."

"It was a true statement," Tushenkov explained. "We have no active work here in Roswell, but we still own these old buildings."

"And maybe that white pickup truck, over there?" Roger nodded in the direction of truck that had sideswiped their rental car on the road from Santa Fe.

Tushenkov shrugged. "It may be assigned to the security staff tasked with keeping an eye on this property. They don't like strangers snooping about. But before we go inside—" Tushenkov paused. "—you do want to go inside, don't you?"

"Of course," offered Amanda.

"Why don't you introduce your—friend?"

"Certainly. How rude of me. Doctor Tushenkov, this is Professor Roger Atwood, Chairman of the History Department at Gettysburg College. Doctor Tushenkov is the Technical Director of Wormstone Engineering. He was kind enough to allow me to interview him back in Washington." The two men shook hands. Tushenkov then removed a large ring of keys from his jacket pocket and motioned for the pair to follow him.

Inside, Tushenkov lifted one corner of the dusty canvas tarp and pulled it back, revealing several jagged sections of a metallic rib-like structure covered in black sheathing; all the pieces arranged together to form what vaguely resembled the wing of some strange aircraft.

As Tushenkov walked along the length of the shattered and crudely reconstructed wing toward the still-shrouded fuselage near where Roger and Amanda were standing he commented, "The technicians who pieced this craft together did a fairly credible job, considering it was done back in 1947 and '48. Does it look familiar or might it be extra-terrestrial? What do you think?"

"I couldn't say," offered Professor Atwood. Without further comment, Tushenkov grasped another corner of the tarp and threw it back, this time uncovering a shattered transparent windscreen and the angular surfaces of the fuselage near the nose of the craft. The large open port at the root of the wing could be nothing other than an air intake. Roger immediately recognized its distinctive parallelogram shape. "Oh, my!"

CHAPTER TWENTY-EIGHT

"SO TELL ME, MR. BRADY, what prior work experience do you have?" The personnel manager at Wormstone Engineering was interviewing applicants for service and maintenance positions. Ev had responded to an employment ad in the local paper.

"Just odd jobs, since I got out of school."

"Where did you serve during the war?" Ev had to be careful here. He knew that employers—especially those with government contracts—typically checked with the Defense Department to help screen employees. As Everett Brady, he had no military experience.

"I tried to enlist when I turned eighteen, but couldn't pass the physical." Ev could think of no other plausible reason why a man of his age would have missed a hitch in the military during the last war. "They said I had a heart murmur, but I haven't noticed any impact on my life. I'm in pretty good shape, I think."

"Well, Mr. Brady. Our Courier Department is in need of a driver. We could start you at eighty dollars a week. You would be running small parcels and documents between here and Roswell Field and occasionally to Alamogordo or White Sands. You'll need a security clearance. You don't have anything in your background that would nix that, do you?"

"No, sir."

"Ever been arrested? Drunk driving or anything like that?"

"No."

"Well—it shouldn't be a problem then. We can grant you a preliminary confidential clearance to start work based on my determination that you appear to be trustworthy and of good character. The Feds will conduct a background check and we'll have a final determination in about three weeks. Do you want the job?"

"Yes, sir."

"You start Monday morning. Work begins at seven AM. Be here on time, please. We work until four. Lunch break is 11:30 to 12:30."

EV WAS WORRIED about the background check. It wasn't that he feared that the investigation of Everett Brady would turn up something untoward; it was that it wouldn't turn up any record of Everett Brady at all. But he figured the worst that could happen was that he would lose his job. In the mean time, he would have some money coming in—very important as his stash of cash was running low. Ev had spent $700 on a used Chevrolet sedan purchased from the dealer where he had stopped on his first day in town. He had also rented a small two bedroom house at the edge of town for ninety dollars a month.

When Ev reported for his first day of work at the Wormstone Engineering office on Monday morning, the personnel manager introduced him to another courier, Thomas Lightfoot. Thomas greeted Ev with a big smile and a firm and vigorous handshake. He was a big man, belying his name.

"Thomas is making a run to Alamogordo Army Air Field this morning. I want you to ride along. It's less than four hours away, so you should be back by quitting time."

The courier vehicle was an Army Ford pickup truck, painted olive drab with some Army ID numbers in white lettering on the doors. By the time they passed the Roswell city limit sign on U.S. Route 70, Ev had already learned that Thomas Lightfoot was an ex-Marine who had seen action at Guadalcanal, has worked at Wormstone for eighteen months and was married and had a six-month old daughter.

Thomas liked to talk, especially about himself. When Ev asked about their destination, he learned that they wouldn't be visiting the Alamogordo atomic bomb test site.

"Trinity Site is still off limits for anyone without a Top Secret Clearance," Thomas explained. "The Army air base nearby—where we're headed—was a training field for bomber crews during the war. They almost shut the whole place down a year ago, but then they started doing some missile development work and testing. Rumor has it that it's going to become part of the new Air Force Matériel Command. I hear they are going to recommission the place with the name 'Holloman Air Force Base'."

Despite the heat of the day and no air conditioning in the truck, Ev was still enjoying the ride. Maybe it was because the stress that accompanied his test pilot work and the plan to compromise his loyalty that never came to fruition no longer occupied his immediate consciousness. Maybe it was because he had landed the job. It was true that he was going to miss his flying career, but there was always a chance that he would have some opportunity to fly again in the future. But if he could be honest with himself, he would admit that the only real craving from his past came from the beckoning call of the Las Vegas gaming tables.

When Thomas pulled up to the Main Gate at Alamogordo Army Air Field, the armed guard approached the open driver's window and looked in. Thomas handed him the wrapped courier package and then a clipboard for the guard to sign as having received it. The guard then waved them forward and Thomas made a U-turn and drove out the exit lane.

"Is that all there is to it?" asked Ev. "You just drive for four hours, deliver the package, and then drive back?"

"Yeah, that's about it. What did you expect—a personal thank you from the Commanding Officer?"

"No, I just thought we might get a chance to look around and see some old—I mean—some airplanes."

"Not today. But we can go into town and get some lunch before we head back."

The radio in the truck crackled just as Thomas turned on to North White Sands Boulevard in Alamogordo. He picked up the handset. "This is Wormstone Courier Number Three. Thomas Lightfoot speaking, over."

"Hi, Thomas. Have you completed the delivery? Over."

“Yessir. We were about to stop for lunch in town.”

“Make it a long lunch. Don’t plan on getting back here before seven. Lieutenant Hedrick is bringing in some crash wreckage. The Army brass wants it stored at Abe’s Auto Repair next door and we have been given explicit instructions that most civilian personnel are to be sent home on Administrative Leave. Only uniformed personnel will be allowed in the immediate area during the unloading process.”

“Are we going to get overtime for this? Over.”

“Don’t worry about it, Thomas. Over and out.”

CHAPTER TWENTY-NINE

IT WAS EXACTLY THREE WEEKS after his first day of work at Wormstone Engineering in Roswell that Everett Adams—now Everett Brady—was summoned to the employment office. The personnel manager was waiting for him along with a well-dressed gentleman that Ev did not know.

"Everett, this is Agent Randolph from the FBI. He has a few questions regarding your security clearance."

"Certainly. Ask anything you'd like."

"For starters, Mr. Brady, on your employment application you stated that you were born in Caldwell, Texas, on 1 July 1923."

"That's correct."

"Unfortunately, we have been unable to find any official record of that."

"You know, I have had that identity problem all the while growing up. It's because the County Courthouse burned down in 1928 and all the records were lost."

"Yes, we know about the fire and the lost records. The point is that we have been unable to place you in Caldwell at all. There isn't even a record of you graduating from Caldwell High."

"Well, I didn't say I graduated on the application. My school record was pretty spotty."

"And you didn't list an address for your parents."

"That's because I don't know where they are now. I didn't get along with my dad. My parents left the State before the war. I think they might have moved to Florida, but I don't know for sure."

"There must be someone—a friend or maybe a girl friend—that we can interview to help establish your identity."

Ev was concerned now. He didn't expect that the security background check would be so thorough, considering that the war was over and the coming cold war with the Soviets had not yet officially begun. He decided to try projecting a less defensive attitude.

"Well I'm not a goddamn spy or anything—or a Commie."

"Nobody is making such an accusation, Mr. Brady."

"And you didn't find any criminal history on me, did you?"

"No, we didn't. We would just like to interview someone who knew you in Texas."

Ev knew he needed to come up with a name or a plausible reason for why he couldn't. He paused for a minute before replying. "My best friend growing up was a kid named George Anderson. He graduated from high school in Caldwell and enlisted in the Navy. We lost contact after that, but if you can locate him, he can tell you all about me."

Agent Randolph stood up. The interview was over. "We'll look into this George Anderson fellow. He should have a war record. In the meantime, you can continue your work here with the provisional clearance. We'll let you know what we find."

During the next two weeks, Agent Randolph would verify that George Anderson did indeed graduate from Caldwell High School in June 1941 and enlisted in the Navy immediately after the Japanese attack on Pearl Harbor. But there would be no FBI interview of the man. Navy records showed that after flight training, George Anderson was assigned to the carrier *Hornet.* He was lost at sea during the Battle of Midway on June 4, 1942. Of course, this finding of the FBI investigation was exactly what Ev Adams had expected.

After receiving the final investigative report from the FBI, the personnel manager again called Ev to his office. "I'm sorry to tell you, Everett, but your friend George Anderson was lost at Midway, so the FBI wasn't able to proceed further with your final clearance. The good news, however, is that because there were no negatives in your report, you can continue to work here with the provisional clearance pending receipt of any new information. Congratulations."

"I'm sorry to hear about George. He was a good friend."

CHAPTER THIRTY

SUZANNE MARSHALL-JONES was hired by the new Administration's Justice Department three weeks before Inauguration Day. After losing her State Department job four years earlier, she had been working in the DC area for an immigration law firm, but was happy to get back into government service. She found her new position as liaison between the FBI and U.S. Attorney's Office far more challenging than preparing and submitting applications for permanent visas and green cards on behalf of wealthy foreign nationals.

It had been two years since her older sister, Amanda Marshall, had disclosed to her the details of the investigation that she and Roger Atwood had conducted on behalf of Rose Booth, the mother of the naval aviator who had returned, purportedly after 35 years captivity in Vietnam. Suzanne had sat wide-eyed as her sister related the story, but what had captivated the young lawyer most of all were the facts surrounding the two history volumes that had been discovered in the New York City pawnshop, and above all, the missing third volume. Roger had loaned her Volume Two of the series that showed the year 2035 copyright notice.

At Suzanne's request, Amanda had contacted Nathaniel Booth and made arrangements for the two to meet. During an interview with the flyer, it was established that a large trust fund naming him and/or his parents as beneficiaries may have been misappropriated by persons unknown sometime after Khronos Trust Services was dissolved in 1978. This disclosure provided Suzanne with the legal justification she needed to probe deeper into the Booth affair.

With the help of Roger and Amanda, she compiled a list suspects, including Lydia McCabe, the last Khronos employee, Lester Rathburn, the manager at the Flat Iron building in New York City and James Stafford, an officer at the bank in New York. Suzanne believed that one of these individuals was working with the mysterious Asian woman who had purchased the third volume of the book from the New York City pawnshop.

"DO I NEED A LAWYER?" Mai Tran posed the question to the FBI agent who had just begun interviewing her. She had come voluntarily to the FBI office on the 23rd Floor of the Federal Plaza Building in Manhattan. Suzanne Marshall-Jones was monitoring the interview by closed circuit television from an adjoining room.

"This interview is just part of a preliminary investigation, Ms. Tran. It is your right to have your attorney present if you wish. You should know that the Bureau considers you a 'Person of Interest' in a securities fraud investigation related to your activities during your bank employment in New York City."

"It's been several months since I left my job at the bank."

"The investigation is concerned about events of two years ago or more."

"Are you questioning anyone else from the bank?"

"Is there someone else from your bank we should be speaking with?"

"Well, yes, perhaps. You might want to speak with my supervisor, James Stafford." The agent dutifully scribbled Stafford's name on his notepad. But unknown to Mai Tran, Stafford had been questioned the day before in the very same interview room.

"What can you tell me, Ms. Tran, about the disposition of some financial instruments held by the Booth Family Trust at your bank?" Before Mai Tran could answer, the agent pulled his phone from the inside jacket pocket of his suit coat and read the text message that had just been sent to him. "Excuse me. I'll be back shortly to continue this." The agent rose from his chair and abruptly exited the interview room.

SUZANNE MARSHALL-JONES had sent the pre-arranged text message to the interviewing agent as a signal to leave the interview room. She would take over, but didn't want to enter the room immediately. Suzanne wanted to give Mai Tran some time to think about her situation and see what might be learned from the young woman's body language.

It was obvious from the closed circuit television feed that Mai Tran was nervous; she repeatedly pulled at the hair behind her right ear, and her anxiety level seemed to grow with each passing minute that she was left alone in the interview room. After several minutes Suzanne entered the room and introduced herself.

"Hello Ms. Tran. May I call you 'Mai'?"

"Most people just call me 'Mai Tran'."

"Very well. My name is Suzanne Marshall-Jones. I'm with the Justice Department. I will turn off the camera and recorder for this part of the interview so that we might have a candid conversation. Is that all right with you?"

"Yes, that's fine." Mai Tran clasped her hands together as Suzanne seated herself in the agent's chair.

"You should know, Mai Tran, that over the last several days my agents have been pouring over subpoenaed financial records and email messages belonging to your supervisor at the bank, James Stafford." Mai Tran closed both eyes for a moment. "Besides providing evidence of probable wrongdoing by Mr. Stafford in the matter of the Booth Family Trust, these records appear to implicate one other employee from the bank." Suzanne deliberately paused for several seconds. "You know who that other employee might be?"

"Yes, yes I do," Mai Tran answered in a despondent tone.

"We are prepared to issue a subpoena for your banking records, but perhaps that won't be necessary—if you cooperate in this investigation."

"What do you want to know?"

"Tell me exactly what you and Mr. Stafford did and spare no details." Suzanne pushed back from the table between the two women, folding her arms in front of her as Mai Tran began to tell her story.

CHAPTER THIRTY-ONE

"ALL THIS TOOK PLACE a few years back, so please excuse me if I don't have all the details exactly right. James—that is, Mr. Stafford—asked me to help with a new project the bank had been assigned: we were to conduct an asset search on behalf of the Secretary State, trying to locate any abandoned assets for hundreds of New York corporations whose corporate registrations had lapsed. We were told that the purpose was to see that the rightful owners received any lost assets to which they were legally entitled. It was Mr. Stafford's opinion that the real motive was to bring in revenue to help balance the State's budget. If assets were identified, but no owner could be found, they would become State property. We spent months on the project, and the bank earned a percentage fee for everything that was found."

"How much money was involved here?" Suzanne unfolded her arms and raised one hand up to her chin after posing the question.

"For ninety percent of the companies, zero. But in a few cases, there were some substantive amounts. We were able to deliver maybe three million in cash, stocks and real estate to some awfully surprised owners or their heirs and maybe twelve million more to the State of New York. We were surprised to learn that some assets were being held in the Trust Department—Mr. Stafford's department—at our very own bank.

Beneficiaries were found for several of the smaller trust instruments. But there was a large one that had been transferred to our bank years earlier from an investment firm called Khronos Trust Services. It was worth about eight million with the beneficiary listed as Nathaniel Booth.

When we searched the document archives for some clues as to who this individual might be, we found that there had previously been a second trust naming Nathaniel's parents, Rose and her husband—I don't recall his first name—as beneficiaries. The assets of this trust had been distributed to the Booths sometime during the 1960s.

With a little detective work, I was able to locate the right Rose Booth in Richmond, but by then our contract with the State had expired and James told me to take no further action. I kept asking him when we were going to notify Rose, but he kept putting me off. Finally, I took it upon myself to send her a gold pin that we had found in one of the archive folders. I thought it might have some sentimental value for her."

"This was the Navy pilot's gold pin?"

"Yes, but how did you know that?"

Suzanne folded her arms in front of her once again. "Surely you must know, Mai Tran, that it was Nathaniel Booth who came to us, charging possible fraud by your bank that initiated this entire investigation."

"I guess I should have known."

"So, what happened next?"

"When James found out what I had done, he was livid. It was then he told me that the bank would be in big trouble if we disclosed the existence of a trust that the bank had been sitting on for all these years. He said we should just keep the money. Rose was old and wealthy and didn't need it and Nathaniel had died in Vietnam, thirty-five years earlier. I didn't argue with him. But when Rose called our bank a few days later, we didn't know what to do.

Curiously, she didn't call about any missing money. She wanted information about Khronos Trust Services and anyone connected with it. She was trying to uncover some information about her son, Nathaniel. James put her off for a few days, but soon we were visited by this couple—I guess Rose had hired them."

"That would be Professor Atwood and Amanda Marshall?"

"That's correct. They asked a lot of questions about Khronos Trust. James believed it was all bullcrap—just a cover; that they were really interested in finding out if there was more cash lying around that belonged to Rose. I just wasn't sure. But just to be on the safe side, James had me follow the couple around for the next few days. I was in the sports bar watching them as the news about Nathaniel Booth, the MIA Navy pilot, was first reported."

"What is your opinion of the story? I'm sure you've heard the rumors that the pilot spent years living in the nineteenth century."

"It's pretty hard to believe. I don't know what to think about it."

"Well, I guess you would first need to believe that it was possible to travel back and forward in time." Suzanne moved as close to Mai Tran as the table between them would permit before continuing. "That might be hard to swallow unless you had some evidence that it had actually occurred."

"What kind of evidence?"

"Like, maybe a book from the future?"

Mai Tran turned her eyes away from Suzanne. "You know about the Vietnamese world history book?"

"Yes, we know all about it. Amanda and Professor Atwood were at the same pawnshop the day after you were there and found the first two volumes. Can you confirm to me that there have been several world events that you read about—that were foretold—in Volume Three of the book before they occurred?"

"Yes, several historical events."

"This is very interesting, Mai Tran. I want to hear all about it. I also want to make it clear that we are going to need two things from you if you want to stay out of Federal prison. One, you must agree to testify against James Stafford, your supervisor at the bank. And two, you need to bring that book to me."

CHAPTER THIRTY-TWO

THE EARLIEST IDENTIFIABLE tribal group inhabiting the Las Vegas Valley was the Paiute. They lived in an area known as Big Springs where a natural aquifer brought water to the surface. Today the area is part of the Las Vegas Springs Preserve located west of Downtown Las Vegas.

The Paiutes occupied the region beginning about 700 A.D., migrating seasonally between Big Springs in the winter and nearby mountains during the hot summers. The evidence of their existence can still be found today in Petroglyphs—the surface carvings in rock often depicting people and animals.

The first non-native explorer to visit the Las Vegas Valley was the American, Jedediah Smith, but it was one Rafael Rivera on a Mexican trade mission to California who named the region Las Vegas—meaning "The Meadows" in Spanish—for the grassy area fed by the natural artesian water wells. The abundant supply of water would make Las Vegas a natural stopover location for travelers passing through the region.

In anticipation of the likelihood of war with Mexico, the Tyler Administration sent the John Fremont party to the Las Vegas Valley in 1844. A fort was established there despite the fact that all of Nevada was still part of Mexico at the time. The entire region came under U.S. sovereignty after the Treaty of Guadalupe Hidalgo was signed in 1848, ending the war with Mexico.

A party of Mormon missionaries became the first American settlers in the Las Vegas Valley. They arrived in 1855 but returned to Utah two years later due to difficulty raising crops in the summer heat. But eventually, more and more settlers came into the area and stayed.

Nevada was admitted to the Union in October 1864 while the Civil War was still raging. Statehood had come just three years after it officially became a U.S. Territory. It has been suggested that Statehood came early in order satisfy the financial needs of the Federal Government to fight the Civil War using the hard currency provided by Nevada's gold and silver mines. More likely, it was a political decision to help assure a Republican victory in the 1864 reelection of President Lincoln by adding an additional slate of Republican electors.

The Mormon influence on Las Vegas had been established with the early missionary settlement. It was strengthened with the completion of an important railroad link between Salt Lake City and Southern California with Las Vegas as a key stopover point. The City of Las Vegas was officially founded in 1905.

HISTORICALLY, FEDERAL LAWS have permitted each of the states to determine the legality of gambling activity within their jurisdiction. During the 1800s, lotteries and other forms of gambling became popular in the U.S. and a few cities including New Orleans, San Francisco and Galveston, were for a time known for their gaming activity. But by the early twentieth century, virtually every state in the Union passed laws making gambling illegal. Consequently, gambling in America became an underworld activity, often controlled by the Mafia and other crime syndicates. For these organizations gambling was a natural addition to the illegal consumption of alcohol in speakeasies that sprung up all over the country after Prohibition.

In Nevada, the construction of the Boulder Dam on the Colorado River outside Las Vegas had a great impact on the future of the City as a gaming center. The dam project which began in 1931 soon resulted in a five-fold increase in the population of Las Vegas.

The all-male labor force naturally sought out local entertainment, contributing greatly to economic growth of the City. This contribution was duly noted by the State Legislature and gambling was legalized so that state and local government law enforcement would no longer be at odds with commercial gaming interests. With the completion of the dam in 1935 and the virtually limitless supply of electrical power that became available to the City, more and more brightly-lit hotel-casinos appeared on the Las Vegas skyline. The El Rancho Vegas was the first to be erected along what would eventually be known as the Las Vegas Strip. In 1946 a crime syndicate led by Bugsy Siegel and Meyer Lansky built the Flamingo using funds believed to have been laundered through local banks.

BY MID-JULY 1948 Everett Brady had completed his first full year of employment as a courier for Wormstone Engineering in Roswell, New Mexico, and had earned a week of paid vacation. He had worked hard and saved some money and could no longer ignore the pull from that city in Nevada that had occupied so much of his former life. He had read about the newly built Flamingo Hotel and Casino in Las Vegas and made a reservation for himself for five nights at the hotel.

Although his coworkers cautioned against making the drive in the summer heat and recommended taking the train from Santa Fe instead, Ev would not even consider it. He wanted to be able to get around town on his own after arriving in Las Vegas. He set off before dawn on Saturday morning, spent that night at a cheap motel in Flagstaff and arrived in Las Vegas well before dark on Sunday. The trip was uneventful.

Ev drove north along the two-lane Arrowhead Highway—eventually to become known as Las Vegas Boulevard and much later "The Las Vegas Strip" for that portion of the highway closest to downtown.

There were few landmarks that he could recognize from his 1982 familiarity with the City. Ev had previously assumed that much of Las Vegas had been built up during the 30s and 40s, so he was somewhat surprised to see so many large parcels of vacant land offered for sale. On two such parcels the developer had erected signs proclaiming the sites as "future home" of the Sands Hotel and Casino in one case and the Sahara on another. On neither of the sites had any construction actually begun.

When Ev arrived at the Flamingo on the east side of the highway, he decided to drive further north for a while rather than turning in. He was looking for casinos he had played in previously. When he reached Freemont Street downtown, Ev made a U-turn, returned to the Flamingo and checked in.

CHAPTER THIRTY-THREE

ROGER ATWOOD PHONED Marjorie Hedrick only hours after he and Amanda had been shown the crash wreckage at the Wormstone building annex on Y.O. Road. The new revelation pointed unmistakably to a convergence-related event being somehow responsible for the 1947 Roswell Incident, and Marjorie agreed to see them the next day. Roger was thinking out loud as they drove to the Hedrick home on West Pine Lodge Road.

"We should have considered this explanation from the beginning."

"What are you talking about, Roger?"

"I'm talking about the crash wreckage that we saw at the Wormstone facility yesterday. After your first interview with Doctor Tushenkov back in Washington—when he told you he knew Nathaniel Booth—we should have suspected that the Roswell Incident might be explained by the same sort of phenomenon that the airmen Booth and Hayes experienced."

"That's true," offered Amanda. "That's probably the only reason why he is here in Roswell now."

Once inside the Hedrick home, Roger and Amanda had some more questions for Marjorie Hedrick.

"THANK YOU FOR SEEING US again, Mrs. Hedrick."

"I hope that I can help. And please—call me Marjorie."

"Very well. First, I should tell you that Amanda and I were at the Wormstone facility on Y.O. Road again yesterday. We were inside one of the buildings—the one you called the 'Wormstone Annex'—and saw the crash wreckage recovered back in 1947. As you suggested earlier, that was no alien spacecraft. It was an American Air Force plane from a time much later than 1947—maybe from the 80s or 90s." Roger continued, "From some previous research work on a similar incident, we think we understand how that may have occurred. We were hoping that you might be able to fill in some of the details."

Roger and Amanda couldn't help but notice a pained expression immediately appear on the face of their host, and in a repetition of what had occurred just two days earlier, a man's voice called out from the back of the home. "Marjorie, can you come in here, please?" Marjorie Hedrick excused herself and left her two guests in the living room.

Roger and Amanda could not make out the words of the whispered exchange coming from the rear of the home. They looked at each other, now both believing that once again Marjorie was being cautioned by her brother not to offer up any information they were seeking. The indiscernible exchange went on for several minutes and then abruptly stopped. Marjorie returned to the living room; this time slowly pushing a wheelchair occupied by an elderly gentleman. Roger immediately stood up as Marjorie introduced the man in the chair.

"This is Everett Adams. He's not my brother. He's a—a close friend. He was the pilot of that aircraft—the airplane wreckage that you saw yesterday. His plane crashed in 1947."

"Let's make sure we give them the correct information, Marjorie." The old man raised his right hand and forearm from his lap. Amanda noticed that both of the man's hands were shaking slightly. "When I took off that day of the crash, the year was 1982." The old man wondered why his statement elicited little reaction from the visitors. "If you don't believe me, I can give you details."

"And we want to hear them," offered Amanda.

"Certainly. I think it's time to tell the whole story." Everett looked squarely at Amanda. "You don't seem to me to be the typical crackpot UFO researchers who have descended on this town year after year since 1947. And yet you believe me when I tell you that 1982 suddenly became 1947 for me? Without even raising an eyebrow?"

"Fair question, Mr. Adams," remarked Amanda. "I am sure you recall the news story from three years ago about Nathaniel Booth, the Vietnam-era airman who was shot down in 1968 and came out of the jungle thirty-five years later?"

"Of course. It was a big story in the press. We all heard about it."

Roger interrupted, “Are you sure, Amanda, that we should be talking about this?”

“Yes, Roger, we should. If we wait for permission from some government bureaucrat, we may be waiting forever.” She redirected her attention from Roger and back to the man in the wheelchair. “Nathaniel Booth was not held captive in Vietnam for thirty-five years. The truth is that his entire experience was probably not unlike what you experienced in 1982. The scientific types have labeled the phenomenon a ‘Convergence Event’. When Roger and I started this last investigation, we had no idea that a similar circumstance could be responsible for the Roswell Incident—at least, not until yesterday.”

Everett Adams had a thoughtful expression on his face. “So you’re telling me that my experience was not entirely unique.”

“That’s correct, but we’re anxious to hear all about yours.”

Ev Adams grasped Marjorie Hedrick’s hand. “Marjorie, you’ve been the most important part of my life for the last sixty years. You know how I got here, but there are some things—things that I am not very proud of—that you don’t know.”

DURING THE NEXT TWO HOURS Everett Adams recounted the events of his life beginning with his work as a test pilot during development of the F-117A Nighthawk at the Lockheed Skunkworks at Groom Lake. He told of his addiction to gambling and how he was recruited by a Soviet agent to deliver the super secret airplane into Soviet hands. Ev described the symptoms of the apparent malfunction of his aircraft during his last mission and how he parachuted to safety.

He explained how his mind began to process the steady cascade of evidence that he was no longer living in 1982 as he rode into the small town of Roswell that fateful morning. At one point he wondered if maybe he was dead and that everything he was experiencing was some sort of after-death spiritual illusion. He explained that once he could no longer deny the truth to himself, how thankful he was that the very event that had thrust him back to 1947 would result in the disruption of the espionage plot; the plot in which he had previously agreed to participate. And with his eventual acceptance of what had happened, how he looked forward to getting on with his new life, starting with the simple courier job at Wormstone Engineering.

Everett asked Marjorie for a glass of water. When she returned with it, he continued his story. "I met Marjorie during my second week at Wormstone. She was working in the billing office. I was interested from the start . . ." Ev paused for a moment and smiled at Marjorie; she lovingly reciprocated. ". . . but when I asked one of the guys in the motor pool about her, I was told that she was married to an officer from the base. That meant she was strictly off limits. But we became friends and had a chance to talk from time-to-time. Later that year she told me that her husband had new orders: he was being transferred to some airbase in Texas and that she wouldn't be going with him. I asked her to go out with me the day he left town."

Amanda had to ask the question, "Did you ever meet Dieter Hedrick?"

"No, but from what Marjorie has told me, I think I would have liked the man." Everett paused for a moment when he saw that Marjorie was nodding in agreement. "Employees dating each other was frowned upon, but we began seeing one another anyway. Some months later Marjorie received a small inheritance when her dad passed away, and she bought this house from her landlord. I wanted to move in, but life was different in 1949; she wouldn't hear of it."

Amanda found Everett's life history with Marjorie interesting, but she had questions about Wormstone and the 1947 incident and she sensed that Roger had some of his own. Roger posed the first question.

"Did you or Marjorie ever see the reconstructed Nighthawk in the Wormstone Annex building?"

"I didn't," offered Marjorie. "I remember Dieter telling me that the pieces he recovered were pretty unusual, but I never actually saw any of it; just the tarp-covered wreckage on the day it was brought in."

"Nor did I," added Everett. "Access to that building was pretty restricted, and I never had clearance for it."

"But you knew it was there all along?"

"Sure. At some point after we were together, Marjorie told me about the day that Dieter brought the crash wreckage in. She said there were rumors about it being alien. I told her it wasn't true—that it was probably the pieces of my Nighthawk that were stored in that building."

"Do you think Dieter knew what it was?"

Marjorie spoke up. "Dieter left town before the reconstruction team had finished their work, so I don't know if—"

Everett Adams interrupted her. “Remember that Dieter was an Air Force Colonel before he retired. He probably learned about the F-117 program and saw photos of the plane long before any information was released to the public. The airframe of the Nighthawk is pretty unique looking. Dieter may not have known how it got there, but at some point—maybe by 1990 or so—he surely came to understand that it was a Nighthawk Stealth Fighter that he had recovered back in 1947. I’d guess that Dieter was about to tell you that just before he died.”

Ev’s voice was clearly becoming more strained. His last few sentences had come out at slightly above a whisper and Marjorie brought him another glass of water. Amanda expressed her concern for his condition. “Do you want to stop for today and get some rest, Mr. Adams? We’re very interested in your story, but we could come back later to hear the rest.”

“No, No. I’ll be fine. My throat was a little dry, but it’s better now. Besides, there’s a lot more to tell you.” He paused for a moment to collect his thoughts.

“Just when things were going well with Marjorie, I started thinking about my old bad habit and started making more frequent trips to Las Vegas. Marjorie came along once in a while, but mostly I went by myself. It was all about the gambling.”

“But you could have become a wealthy investor, each year knowing what successful products or properties were under development.” Amanda wondered why Everett was unable to capitalize on his unique opportunity to make a financial success of his life. She had noticed an older compact sedan in the garage when she and Roger pulled into the driveway earlier that day. Inside the house, the furniture and appliances were dated. It appeared that Everett Adams and Marjorie Hedrick had lived a barely comfortable life; there was no evidence of any real wealth here. Ev seemed to sense what Amanda had been thinking.

"I dabbled in the markets some, but other than some IBM stock that I bought early on, I never made much money. I was still a kid growing up in the sixties and too much into my career and having a good time in the seventies to pay much attention to what was going on in business and the economy. I guess I didn't learn very much living through that period that I could use to my advantage the second time through. And of course I no longer had that crystal ball to tell me what was coming after 1982. But I did make some real money once on a land deal."

Roger noticed a broad grin appear suddenly on Everett's face. As soon as his words were out, Marjorie folded her arms in front of her and looked down at the living room floor. She clearly did not approve of the story that Ev was about to tell, but he continued.

"The Sands Hotel and Casino wasn't built yet, so the Flamingo became my casino of choice. There was a large parcel of vacant land catty-corner from the hotel at the intersection of Flamingo Road and the Vegas Strip. I knew that eventually, the Dunes Resort would be built on that piece of ground. One weekend, I had a terrific winning streak at the tables—made eleven thousand dollars—one of my best ever. Before I left town, I called the phone number on the For Sale sign on that property. Marjorie and I returned to Vegas the next weekend and plunked down ninety-five hundred dollars in return for a three year option on the property. Sold it to the developer for a hundred grand two years later. They built the hotel in 1955 and later tore it down and built a new one—the Bellagio—on that site."

Roger made the comment, "A hundred thousand dollars? That was a lot of money in the 1950s."

"Sure was. Marjorie and I were living high for a long time. Bought a brand new '55 T-Bird. It was yellow. I loved that car! And I got a great deal on a light plane, a Piper Super Cub. We did a lot of traveling in that plane over the years. But it didn't last. Eventually I lost my edge. I was losing more than I was winning, but I couldn't stay away from the tables. Our savings dwindled. By 1982, all we had left was this house and an old car. Marjorie threatened to leave me several times. Eventually she did. She wouldn't come back until I promised to give up gambling and never go back to Las Vegas."

Marjorie added, "And he never has since that day, thank God."

"No. Thank *you*, Marjorie. I only wish that my gambling habit had never followed me to Roswell."

Roger was considering something that Everett Adams had mentioned previously and had another question. "Before the crash in Roswell in 1982, when you were working at Groom Lake, you said you did a lot of gambling in Las Vegas."

"Correct."

"And then after the crash you traveled there quite often up until 1982?"

"Yes, that's right."

"So that means that Everett One, the test pilot, could have been in Las Vegas at the exact same time that Everett Two, the former Wormstone courier, was there?"

"Yes, that is true. And I know what you are about to ask me next: Was there ever an encounter between me and myself? Between Everett One and Everett Two?"

"Yes," replied Roger. "That's the question."

"My last trip to Las Vegas, post-crash, was in April 1982. I hadn't been back for months and didn't go there with poker on my mind. I went there—you might say—to convince my former self that the plan to deliver my airplane to the Russians and defect was a particularly reckless and stupid idea. I hadn't learned a great deal in the previous thirty-five years, but maybe a few lessons of life had stuck.

I had played the tape of the conversation I would have with myself over and over again in my head, and I was ready to deliver it. But when I was still a few blocks from the Sands Casino, I started feeling nauseous. And as I drove closer, my head started to ache. It was a migraine—so painful that I could no longer drive. I pulled over and it was then I remembered the only other time I had experienced similar pain. It was thirty-five years earlier, sitting at the casino bar, just after Leo had suggested the way to solve my financial problems."

"You believe that some sort of force was acting on each of you, effectively preventing any face-to-face encounter?"

"I have no other explanation. When I turned the car around and headed away from the casino, I immediately started to recover. By the time I reached the edge of town, the pain was gone."

Marjorie could tell that Everett was very tired and needed to get back to his bed. She reached over and stroked the side of his face. It was clear to Amanda and Roger that the meeting was over. Roger thanked the couple for their time and willingness to share their stories. As they rose to leave, Amanda remembered something she had wanted to ask earlier. She drew near to the man in the wheelchair. "Everett, you said that it was one of the men you played poker with that proposed the conspiracy to turn over your airplane and defect. Is that correct?"

"Yes. It eventually became clear to me that Leo joining in the weekly poker game was no coincidence. That was part of his plan from the beginning, to get close to me."

"You said his name was Leo. As in Leonid?"

"Yes. When he wasn't around, the other players usually referred to him as 'The Russian'. He had a slight accent."

Amanda wondered if maybe she and Roger knew this Leonid, the Russian.

CHAPTER THIRTY-FOUR

AMANDA MADE THE REQUEST before Roger had even begun to back down the driveway after their meeting with Marjorie Hedrick and Everett Adams. "We need to go back to Wormstone Engineering in the morning. I want to take some photos and speak with Doctor Tushenkov again, if we can."

"Why, Amanda? You've got your story."

"You mean our story, don't you?"

"Sure, OK. Our story. But tell me, what more can you possibly learn from Tushenkov?"

"Just a hunch—and a few loose ends that need to be wrapped up."

"As you wish," replied Roger with a mocking theatrical flourish. He raised his right hand to grip the brim of his imaginary chauffeur's cap with thumb and forefinger as if to say, "Yes, ma'am," as he drove off.

THE NEXT MORNING Roger pulled into the parking lot of the main Wormstone Engineering building. An 18-wheeler with a large box trailer was parked behind the Wormstone Annex. The driver had left the engine running, and the door to the cab of his truck was open. Roger thought he recognized the man next to the cab. He carried a briefcase and was speaking with the driver.

"Isn't that your Doctor Tushenkov? How did you know he'd be here?" Without waiting for an answer, Roger parked the Jeep nearby, and he and Amanda exited the vehicle. Tushenkov waved to the couple as they approached. With no apparent urgency, the driver of the semi-truck and trailer pulled the door of his truck closed, released the air brake and pulled slowly out of the parking lot and on to Y.O. Road and drove away.

Roger glanced toward the open bay doorway of the Wormstone Annex building near where they were standing and noted that the crash wreckage present inside just yesterday was nowhere to be seen. "Doctor Tushenkov, we see that you have been busy since we were last here with you."

"Yes. It became necessary to remove the aircraft wreckage from this site before it became a tourist attraction. The truck that just left will be in Groom Lake within twenty-four hours."

"I don't mean to be presumptuous, Doctor, but why is it that you seem to be behind every effort to block our investigation of the Roswell Incident?"

Tushenkov replied to the question, "Why don't we go inside and discuss the entire matter openly? I have some information that I believe you will find most interesting." Roger and Amanda followed Tushenkov to the table and chairs in one corner of the open bay of the Wormstone Annex. He lit a cigarette as they sat down and tossed the pack on the table, briefcase on the floor beside him.

"First, understand that I was very much involved in the NSA investigation of events surrounding the return to 2003 of the airman, Nathaniel Booth. I spent several hours in a debriefing session with Booth during a flight back to the East Coast."

Roger spoke up, "You told Amanda about your involvement with the NSA during her interview with you in your Virginia office. How long had you worked for that organization?"

"Since the mid 1990s and until about one year ago."

Amanda barely waited for Tushenkov to complete his answer when she fired another question at him. "So you weren't working for the NSA when you coerced Everett Adams to commit treason and deliver a super secret U.S. Stealth Fighter into Soviet hands?"

Tushenkov paused before responding to Amanda's unveiled accusation of wrongdoing. "I see that you have been very thorough in your research, Ms. Marshall. When that failed initiative took place in 1982, I was a proud officer in the Soviet KGB. But all that changed with the breakup of the Soviet Union. I went to the U.S. Government—first the CIA—and disclosed all of my previous activities to them. Had the stealth mission with Adams succeeded, I am sure they would have been less accommodating, but as it turned out, the U.S. Government was happy to employ me. I have been loyal to this country ever since. Ten years ago I became a citizen." When there was no immediate response from Amanda, he continued. "And you should know that the NSA has known the whereabouts of Everett Adams for several years. But it has been only recently that they learned, as I have, of his excursion back to 1947."

"What about the murder of Dieter Hedrick. I was there. Before he died, he implicated Wormstone—your company."

"Let me show you something." Dr. Tushenkov opened his briefcase and removed a single sheet of paper on which was printed two police booking photos. He placed the photos on the table. "These were sent to me just this morning. Ms. Marshall, do you recognize this couple?" Amanda picked up the photos and examined them closely.

"Yes. These are the people who came into Dieter Hedrick's room at the hospital and administered the lethal IV. Only the man had short hair and was clean shaven. The woman's hair was much lighter in color."

"You will be happy to know that they were arrested yesterday in Washington D.C. I'm sure you could make a call and confirm this for yourself."

"Who are they and why would they want to keep Colonel Hedrick from talking to me?" Amanda was upset.

"The man is Jeffrey Winslow, a self-proclaimed UFOologist with some history of mental issues. The woman's name is Ruby Stimson. She apparently had some medical experience, but that's all I know about her. Winslow was to be the keynote speaker at the UFO Convention next July here in Roswell. It is an annual affair, every year near the anniversary date of the incident. Apparently, Winslow was obsessed with the fear that Colonel Hedrick's revelation to you would refute the premise of his recently published book and might derail a rumored movie deal."

"And the premise of his book is what?"

Tushenkov responded, "Winslow claims that according to a credible Groom Lake Area 51 veteran connected to Roswell, that the craft that came down in July 1947 was Soviet, on a spy mission. Supposedly, it was developed by captured Nazi scientists, from designs the Germans were working on during the war."

Roger offered a reasonable objection to Tushenkov's explanation. "What is it about that theory that would appeal to the UFO crowd? Certainly not a topic for a UFO convention."

Tushenkov countered, "Let me finish. Apparently, the German designs were based on alien artifacts—a set of obsidian tablets engraved with engineering data uncovered by Nazi soldiers in the North African desert sometime in 1942."

Roger was skeptical. "Sounds to me like the plot for an Indiana Jones movie. What about bodies of the crewmen? If it was a spy mission, there had to be spies aboard."

"He claims that alien-like bodies were found in the crash wreckage. His explanation was that the crew was made up of genetically-engineered humans, bred specifically for the spy mission by—of course—other Nazi scientists."

"Did he intend to offer any proof of his claim, other than the testimony of one individual?"

"The rumor was that he planned to present some of the original alien tablets at the UFO Convention. All this is, of course, a fairy tale. Any tablets he planned to show were likely fabricated in his basement."

Amanda didn't necessarily believe everything that Dr. Tushenkov was telling them, but neither did she have evidence to refute any of it. "OK, Doctor. You have been able to present a plausible explanation for events that conveniently absolves yourself of any recent wrongdoing, but what about the white pickup truck behind the engineering building—the one that nearly ran us off the road when Professor Atwood and I were on our way into town?"

"I asked our Security Supervisor about the truck; it's been here for several days. The truck does not belong to Wormstone. We don't know who it belongs to. The police are checking—maybe it was stolen. Whoever was trying to discourage you and Professor Atwood from your investigation obviously wished to direct your suspicion away from themselves. Wormstone was the logical choice for blame."

Roger and Amanda were having some difficulty processing the cascade of new information they had received in the last few minutes. As they prepared to leave, Roger asked about something that had been bothering him since their last visit yesterday at the home of Marjorie Hedrick.

"Doctor Tushenkov, there is a curious distinction between the series of convergence events associated with Nathaniel Booth and the single event at Roswell. In both cases, thirty-five years lapsed *between* events, but the actual temporal shift in the Booth case was one hundred-and-five years. And unlike Roswell, Nathaniel Booth experienced both a temporal and spatial shift, finding himself in both a different time and place." Tushenkov nodded, acknowledging the veracity of Roger's observation. "Why the difference?"

"I don't know, but I'm told that some NSA scientists are already looking into it. In studying the Booth case, one theory was that a series of lunar and planetary conjunctions might be triggering the events—something gravity-related. If this theory proves correct, gravity variation may be able to account for the differences somehow."

CHAPTER THIRTY-FIVE

AFTER LEARNING that she was a subject in a Justice Department criminal investigation during the interview by Suzanne Marshall-Jones, Mai Tran was scared. There was no way she was going to prison if she could avoid it. No question; she *would* testify against her old boss, James Stafford. But there was a second condition imposed on her if she was to avoid prosecution in the matter of the Booth Trust.

Mai Tran tapped lightly on the door of the apartment in Queens. It was late, but she hoped that her grandmother was still awake. Mai Tran had come to her grandmother's apartment to retrieve the book and deliver it to Suzanne Marshall-Jones.

"Who is it?"

"It's me, Ba Noi. It's Mai Tran."

"Come in, child." Grandmother Linh opened the door. "It is so late, Mai Tran. What do you want? You don't look well. Are you alright?"

"I'm OK. I've just been under a lot of pressure at work. I've come for my book, Grandmother. I need the history book." Grandmother Linh turned away from Mai Tran and looked down at the kitchen floor.

"What is the matter, Grandmother. You still have my book, don't you?"

"I burned it, Mai Tran."

"No. No. It was my book, Grandmother. Why would you destroy it?" The young woman was clearly upset. Grandmother Linh reached out and held Mai Tran's two hands in her own.

Looking directly into her granddaughter's eyes, she spoke. "It is not right, Mai Tran. We must live through the events of our life as they come. Nobody should know the future."

MAI TRAN WAS TERRIFIED with the prospect of disclosing to Suzanne Marshall-Jones that the history book that she promised to deliver had been destroyed. Would Suzanne believe that Grandmother Linh burned it? It sounded more like a fabricated excuse for not wanting to follow through with her commitment. "She has to believe me," Mai Tran told herself. "I can't go to prison."

The next morning, Mai Tran came to Suzanne's office at the Federal Plaza Building in Manhattan. She brought Grandmother Linh with her.

"Ms. Marshall-Jones, this is my Grandmother. We bring some bad news."

CHAPTER THIRTY-SIX

ROGER AND AMANDA left Roswell the day after their last meeting with Leonid Tushenkov. Roger returned to Gettysburg for the start of the winter term; Amanda to her Crystal City condo where she spent the next month working on a three-part magazine article entitled ROSWELL: THE FINAL ACCOUNT. Roger had contributed a lot of technical detail, including a section on stealth technology, and would be cited as a contributing author.

Peter Gleason, Amanda's agent, read the final draft and suggested that maybe the manuscript should be expanded and published as a non-fiction book. "Roswell still captures the imagination of the American public," he argued. "A published book would add credibility to your work and potentially reach a wider audience. I think we could sell a boat-load of books."

Roger spent most of the weekends during the school term with Amanda, commuting between Crystal City and Gettysburg College to teach his history classes during the week. He had decided to take the summer off and by the beginning of August, their book-length manuscript was complete. They did not attend the Roswell UFO Convention that was held in July.

Roswell: the Final Account, by Amanda Marshall and Professor Roger Atwood, was met with mixed reviews. The presented "facts" were considered by many critics to be so far beyond belief that the work was often classified as "pseudo non-fiction." Most of the independent attempts to substantiate the events described in the book were frustrated: Everett Adams died of natural causes in Roswell, New Mexico, just three days before the book was released. He had been sent an advance copy two weeks earlier.

Dr. Leonid Tushenkov resigned as Director of the Wormstone Group in September and was rumored to have returned to a position with the National Security Agency, but could not be located for comment. The U.S. Air Force made no official statement concerning the claims made in the book, but an unidentified Pentagon spokesman calling in to a popular national radio talk show suggested that an earlier theory—the one about the Soviet spy mission and genetically-engineered humans—was a far more plausible explanation for the 1947 Roswell Incident.

Amanda learned from her sister, Suzanne, that Mai Tran was unable to produce the coveted history volume. Suzanne believed the grandmother's explanation of how and why the book had been destroyed and agreed that Mai Tran would not face criminal charges.

With the expectation that Mai Tran would testify against her former supervisor, James Stafford pleaded guilty to fraud charges and was sentenced to ten years in Federal prison. Approximately seventy percent of the funds stolen from the Booth Family Trust by Stafford and Mai Tran were returned to Rose and

Nathaniel Booth. The remaining thirty percent could not be accounted for—most likely spent on lavish vacations and luxuries by Stafford and his assistant.

NEITHER ROGER NOR AMANDA was particularly disappointed by the distinctly lackluster response to their work. It had garnered some loyal followers, and the couple was considering a new research project. They had grown closer—once again—over the summer and both seemed happy about it. Roger just hoped it would last.

AFTERWORD

Publisher's Note: The world history textbook found in a New York City pawn shop by Mai Tran, the administrative assistant at the bank, included a brief account of the secession of the State of Texas from the United States of America. The announcement of secession and subsequent related events—if true—would rank as one of the most significant world news stories to be reported during the twenty-first century.

The following is a detailed account of the facts and circumstances surrounding the secession event. It appears to have been recorded during the month of July, but the year is not specified in the document. According to some analysts, July 2017 is a significant possible date in that it is exactly 35 years from the 1982 disappearance of Everett Adams' Nighthawk over the skies of New Mexico and 70 years after the famous 1947 Roswell crash. However, from the content of the account, all that is known with certainty is that it occurs in the first year of a new Presidential Administration. Some researchers have suggested that 2021 or 2025 is a more likely timeframe.

The document, reprinted below, was sent anonymously to Amanda Marshall at her Arlington, Virginia, home shortly after the release of the book, Roswell: the Final Account. In a footnote not included here, the author concedes that much of the private dialog between the principals presented in the document was added for dramatic effect, but is believed to be consistent with the actual events as they unfolded. The content would suggest that the author—although unknown at this time—was an individual close to several highly placed sources connected to the secession movement. There was no explanation for how the details of this event, set several years in the future, became known to the author.

BY JANUARY, after yet another lackluster holiday merchant selling season, most economists believed that the U.S. could no longer avoid another severe economic downturn. The revisions to the previous quarterly statistics showed that the economy had contracted more than first reported, and talk of secession in some states was once again filling the air and the airwaves.

The latest employment reports revealed that the official unemployment rate was again on a rising trend, and counting those individuals who had given up looking for work, the true figure was over seventeen percent. Within a few weeks after Inauguration Day, the S&P 500 Stock Index closed below 700, nearly touching the intraday low reached on March 9, 2009. At the New York Mercantile Exchange, gold futures for April delivery closed above $2,000 per ounce.

After an emergency meeting of the Organization of Petroleum Exporting Countries (OPEC), it was announced after the close of the New York markets on that day that the price of a barrel of OPEC oil would be fixed for the foreseeable future at the dollar equivalent of one-sixteenth ounce of gold for the same contract delivery month of both commodities. The sixteen-to-one ratio of price for one ounce of gold to one barrel of crude oil was consistent with past historical price data.

The OPEC spokesman from Saudi Arabia argued that this change should help stabilize oil prices worldwide—that is, as long as the stability of the U.S. Dollar could be maintained. The Administration complained bitterly that the new OPEC pricing policy would put one more nail in the coffin that could soon bury the U.S. Dollar as the world's reserve currency.

In concluding an emergency meeting with his economic advisers, the new President summarized the formidable task facing his economic team. "I don't need to tell you that we are accountable for the future direction of this economy. It is always easy to blame the previous administration for lingering economic problems, but I don't want to hear even a suggestion of that coming from anyone in this room. I believe that we can chart a direction that will prove to be successful. Make it happen. If we can't, rest assured that the country won't be giving us another four years to keep trying."

In truth, the economy had been in a general decline for years with only occasional brief periods showing minor improvement before the downtrend continued again. Republicans and Democrats each had turns holding the reigns of power in the Oval Office and Congress, but neither tax cuts nor tax increases, nor more or less government spending, seemed to have a long term, positive impact on either economic growth or government debt reduction. Most voters no longer blamed the President or a single political party in Congress for the continuing economic malaise; they blamed both parties.

The seeds of the problem had long before been planted in Europe. Continuing high levels of sovereign debt that had threatened the weaker members of the European Union eventually came home to roost. Social upheaval in Greece led that country's return to the Drachma, abandoning the Euro, rather than adopting austere measures demanded by stronger members of the Union and the European Central Bank.

Bond interest rates doubled nearly overnight. Spain, Portugal and Ireland defaulted on their sovereign debt. Bank failures in Europe quickly spread across the globe and U.S. banks were not spared from the turmoil. The violence in Iraq and later Afghanistan that had been on the rise since American troop withdrawals that began in 2011 had steadily escalated and eventually spread to Saudi Arabia. World oil prices once again exceeded $150 per barrel; gasoline prices in the U.S. remained above five dollars a gallon. In Europe, Germany had by default gained defacto political and economic control over her remaining Eurozone neighbors; a result—more than one cynical observer remarked—that two World Wars had failed to achieve.

THE "OCCUPY WALL STREET" protesters returned to the streets in the spring. Simultaneous protests sprung up in Chicago, St. Louis, Atlanta, Oakland, Portland, Los Angeles and a dozen other cities. Union protesters in several states called for repeal of "right-to-work" laws. It was claimed that these laws had severely and unfairly curtailed union membership. It was reasonably argued that the low level of union membership in these states had the effect of suppressing wages for even non-union lower and middle class workers.

In California, this labor union complaint was suddenly overshadowed by the vociferous expressions of outrage from California public employee unions when it was learned that State Legislators were seriously considering the option of solving the State's disastrous financial situation through bankruptcy. State Bankruptcy was thought to be the only means whereby employee retirement pensions could be scaled back. Without such drastic action, growth in pensions and retiree healthcare benefits would very soon begin to devour more than two-thirds of future State revenues.

Anarchists made up the second largest segment of protesters. They sounded the usual cry for dissolution of the megabanks and all publicly held corporations, free health care and higher education for all and taking what is needed from the wealthy.

On one Friday afternoon, workers in one of the high rise offices above the street in New York answered the chanting protesters by dumping thousands of blank employment application forms from local fast food establishments on their heads like so much confetti. This less-than-subtle statement of regard was not well received by the crowd below. That very evening a small band of protesters responded to the insult by placing an explosive charge under the tail of the bronze sculpture of the Charging Bull in Bowling Green Park near Wall Street. The blast upended the sculpture and blew off the tail, testicles and one of the rear legs of the seven thousand pound Wall Street Bull.

THE GOVERNORS OF TEXAS and the Mexican State of Tamaulipas were close friends. They had known each other since the Texas Governor first became Lieutenant Governor of Texas four years earlier. In Mexico, Governor Castillo lost his first bid for Governor but ran again and won for a six-year term, beating his National Action Party opponent by a better than two-to-one margin. The two governors and their families often spent vacation time together in Veracruz or Galveston.

But a meeting of the two requested by Castillo barely one day earlier was to be at the Governor's office at the State Capitol in Austin. The Texas Governor quickly agreed to the meeting despite Castillo's unwillingness to disclose in advance his purpose in calling for the one-on-one session.

"Guillermo, I'm pleased that you came here today!" The two men greeted each other with an off-center hug and mutual patting of backs. "What is so urgent that you would come to Austin on such short notice?"

"I need to ask you about the vote of your State Legislature at the end of this month."

"You mean the secession vote?"

"Yes. Will it pass?"

"It's two weeks before the vote; still too early to tell. Passage requires a two-thirds majority of both houses and several Senators from our border districts—including your border—are concerned about security. If the measure passes, they are worried about what kind of response to expect from my Federal government, and from yours."

"And if the measure passes, you will—"

The Texas Governor did not wait for Castillo to finish his question. "If the measure passes, I will sign it."

"What if I told you that I could reduce the threat to Texas from the Mexican government?"

"You have that much influence with the power in Mexico City?" The Texas Governor seated himself in one of the two overstuffed leather easy chairs facing the Governor's desk and motioned for Castillo to do the same.

"No, I don't. In fact, the National Government is quite unhappy with me and most of the other elected officials in Tamaulipas. Tension has existed with Mexico City from long before I was elected to office. We request help controlling the drug cartels but no help is ever forthcoming. Thanks to investment by international companies and growth of the maquiladoras, the standard of living of our citizens has improved enormously. We are in a better economic condition than ever before despite the efforts by Mexico City to curtail our growth with nonsensical commercial regulations and corruption at every level. In many respects, our relationship with our National

Government is not unlike yours here in Texas with the U.S. Federal Government."

"What are you suggesting, Guillermo?"

"As the highest elected official from the State of Tamaulipas, I am here to request that we be permitted to join your secession movement. We want to become a part of the great new Republic of Texas." The Texas Governor raised his hand to cover his eyes as he pondered the implications of the shocking revelation disclosed by his friend. Castillo continued, "Our citizens have far more in common with the people of Texas than with their Mexican brothers."

"The successful secession of Texas will be viewed in Washington—and maybe in the rest of my country—as a national crisis of gigantic proportion. If Tamaulipas were to join us, it would become an international incident."

"I can't disagree," Castillo added. "But now is the right time for such a bold move. There is political and economic chaos in both of our countries. We may never again have such an opportunity as we do now."

HOW TO MOVE THE PRESIDENT'S economic plan forward was the main topic of discussion at the party Leadership Conference in May. Opinions varied widely. Party hardliners insisted that there be no further concessions to the opposition party in the Senate. Moderates argued that failure to pass a plan would be blamed on intransigence of the President's party and could cost them dearly in the next election.

The President addressed the group on the last day of the conference. He concluded his remarks by asking his Governors to be patient. He promised to meet with the leadership of both Congressional parties once again to see what it would take to pass legislation that could get the country moving again.

Upon his return to the White House, the President's Chief of Staff passed the word that the Governor of Texas had come for an unexpected visit and asked for a private meeting.

"IT'S GOOD TO SEE YOU, GOVERNOR." The President extended his hand to the Governor of Texas. "Please sit. What can I do for you today?"

"You've heard of the renewed chatter going on in my state, Mr. President?"

"You mean the renewed talk of secession?"

"Yes sir."

"Well, yes. I believe the whole country has heard about it, don't you think? But it is just talk, isn't it? Like last time?"

"No, sir. It's more than just talk. Our citizens have just about had it with this economy and with the failure of Congress to do anything about it. Our people don't understand why the Federal government wants to take charge of so many aspects of their lives. They are concerned about the latest edicts from unelected officials in the EPA and HHS while doing nothing about issues for which the government has legitimate responsibility—like immigration. It makes absolutely no sense."

"I can understand the frustration you must feel, but you and the conservative citizens of Texas—and the rest of the country, I might add—must accept the fact that the last Congressional elections have consequences. The United States was once a moderately conservative country; we are now moderately progressive. However, you should take some comfort in the fact that the recent legislation passed by the House addresses many of your concerns, including reducing regulations and easing the tax burden."

"In the House, yes, but nobody believes you can get any substantive portion of your economic plan through the Senate. It's as if the most extreme members of Congress on both sides of the aisle have formed a coalition to block passage." The Governor paused before adding, "You need to know that the Texas State Assembly is determined to go forward with a secession vote at the end of next month if no progress is made before then."

The President was visibly irritated. "Are you making a threat, Governor?"

"No, Mr. President. I'm just the messenger. Texans believe that we have been carrying the country for a long time. Our unemployment rate is one of the lowest of all the states, and we would be adding even more jobs if the Federal government would do something to reduce the crushing Federal debt and the regulations that discourage our businesses from expanding. Your Justice Department continues to prosecute their own Border Patrol agents in our state for being too aggressive in interdicting criminal illegal aliens. And I'm referring to criminals engaged in drug trafficking and weapons trade. Our lawmakers in Austin are listening to our people and simply refuse to continue along this unsustainable path."

"Let me remind you that this is the United States of America, not the Eurozone. And it's the twenty-first century, not the nineteenth. We have to stick together and see this thing through. I don't even want to think about having to send Federal troops to Austin."

"I don't believe you would do that, sir."

"Try me. I refuse to be remembered as the first American President since the Civil War to preside over the breakup of the United States." The President called for his Chief of Staff after the Governor left the Oval Office.

"I need you to check with every Department: Find anyone with evidence that this Texas Secession movement is more than just an idle threat."

THE PRESIDENT'S Chief of Staff and the Secretary of Defense were in the hastily assembled meeting with the President. "According to our second-hand source, the announcement is less than two months away and involves not only Texas, but one of the northern states of Mexico is also in play."

"How credible is the source?" asked the President.

"The woman who was the original source cannot be located. She was given immunity many years ago for testifying against her former supervisor. It was a successful prosecution and she seemed fairly credible. Unfortunately, the book that detailed all this was apparently destroyed before we could get our hands on it and there are no copies. But the details of many of the other events she reported that were foretold in the book—particularly about the economic unrest in Europe—have come to pass."

The President turned to his Secretary of Defense. "Put together some sea and air assets. I want you to get a carrier task group into the Western Gulf of

Mexico, just in case. Let's not publicize a big show of force for now, but we may need to do exactly that before long."

"As you wish, Mr. President."

EDUARDO GOMEZ, the Mexican Ambassador to the United Nations, had requested the emergency meeting of the Security Council just one day after the Governor of the Mexican State of Tamaulipas announced that his state intended to join with Texas and become part of the newly formed Republic of Texas.

The UN emergency meeting was opened by the President of the Security Council. For the current month, the UN President's office was held by the non-permanent member from the Republic of Azerbaijan. Contemporaneous translations of the President's opening remarks were heard by all council members.

"This meeting of the Security Council is called to order. The provisional agenda for consideration is the situation in the State of Tamaulipas in Mexico." . . . a pause while the President counted the hands raised in approval of the provisional agenda. . . . "The agenda is adopted. Under Rule 37 of the Council's Provisional Rules of Procedure, I invite the representative of Mexico to participate in this meeting." . . . another pause and another affirmative vote. . . . "It is so decided. I now give the floor to the representative from Mexico."

"Mr. President—your Excellency—distinguished council members, ladies and gentlemen. I come to you today to present the grave concerns of my government over the recent turn of events within the Mexican State of Tamaulipas and the U.S. State of Texas. As you know, in a quick succession of events, representatives of the State of Texas have recently passed a secession vote. If this vote is not overturned by the Congress of the United States and/or possible intervention by U.S. military forces, the Republic of Texas will be permanently established. Let me be clear that my government considers the secession of Texas to be a matter for Texas and the Federal Government of the United States to resolve, and that Mexico has no official position on the matter. We have no interest in interfering with matters internal to the United States. However, the secession was followed by action within the Mexican State of Tamaulipas to join the Texas Republic."

The representative from Mexico continued. "The Mexican government has formally ordered officials from the State of Tamaulipas to reconsider their action and pledge their allegiance to the greater United Mexican States. This order was issued with the promise that with their immediate compliance, there would be no retribution taken against the people or any officials of the State. To underscore the seriousness of this internal matter facing my country, elements of the Mexican Federal Army are now positioned in Nuevo León and San Luis Potosi along the state line of Tamaulipas to assure compliance with the directive from the National Government. But this, too, is not a matter for concern of this great body, the Security Council of the United Nations."

"I am here today to express the outrage of my government to credible evidence that this entire secession affair has been orchestrated by officials high in the U.S. Government for the express purpose of once again stealing territory from Mexico." A loud murmur of astonishment could be heard from many of the members and guests in the Security Council chamber. The President pounded his gavel to restore order. "It is an accepted fact that the United States Government promoted the Texas independence movement in 1836 and the Mexican War of 1846 for the express purpose of adding more than a half-million square miles of Texas and Aztlán—what America calls the Mexican Cession—to the territory of the United States. Now it is their intention to repeat the treachery and steal more land from a country that until this day has been America's most loyal friend. It is a disgrace. Mr. President, I call for a vote of censure of the United States in this matter." Several member representatives of the Security Council responded with applause, including representatives from China and the Russian Federation.

The President pounded his gavel to restore order in the chamber. "Mr. Gomez, we have no pending draft resolution of censure for consideration. Is it your intention to submit such a draft?"

"Ah—yes, Mr. President." The representative from Mexico was unsure of the procedural steps required for a censure vote.

"A vote will be considered upon review of the submitted draft." The U.S. Representative raised his hand and was recognized by the President.

"Mr. President, council members, ladies and gentlemen. The United States has no intention to annex, directly or through any nefarious plan, lands belonging to Mexico. The action taken by the State of

Tamaulipas was not foreseen by my Government; it came as a complete surprise. I can assure you that the United States is making every effort to settle the matter of secession of our State of Texas in a peaceful manner. The entire circumstance has caused a constitutional crisis in my country. We are one-hundred percent engaged in seeking an amicable agreement with our wayward citizens and have neither the time nor the mandate to interfere with an issue internal to Mexico."

Mr. Gomez did not wait to be recognized by the President and heatedly challenged the American. "Then you deny the movement of elements of the Texas National Guard across the border and into the State of Tamaulipas?"

"I am unaware of any such troop movements."

"And do you also deny that your country is about to establish a No-Fly Zone over Texas and Northern Mexico?"

"I have heard of no plans to establish a No-Fly Zone."

"Then is the representative from the United States also unaware that in the last 48 hours, the American aircraft carrier *USS George Washington* has moved into position north of the Bay of Campeche, inside Mexican territorial waters and less than two hundred kilometers east of Veracruz?"

The U.S. Representative covered the microphone with his cupped hand and turned to consult privately with a staffer. He turned back to the Council and made a statement. "I have just been informed that there have been some recent new developments regarding possible deployment of U.S. forces. My staff is gathering the information, and you shall have your answers in due course."

Mr. Gomez smiled broadly before responding. "I am prepared to wait for your answer until hell freezes over, if that is your decision."

THE REPUBLIC OF TEXAS was officially recognized by the U.S. Government and the United Nations on June 15th. It included the former Mexican State of Tamaulipas. Behind-the-scenes diplomacy is generally credited with securing independence for the new republic without a shot being fired.

In a concession to U.S. negotiators, it is rumored that Texas authorities formally agreed to consider readmission to the Union at some unspecified time in the future. According to the rumor, a referendum on readmission will be presented to the citizens of the Texas when a majority vote of the Congress of the Republic certifies that that the U.S. Government has made good on promises to initiate what they determine to be much needed political and economic reforms.

The Government of Mexico has steadfastly refused to officially recognize the Republic of Texas, claiming that it was coerced to give up the State of Tamaulipas under threat of military action by the United States.

ABOUT THE AUTHOR

Thomas Settimi graduated from the Institute of Technology at the University of Minnesota and earned a Master's Degree in Physics from the University of California at Riverside. For much of his professional career he has been engaged in technical writing and engineering for the Department of the Navy and defense-related firms.

Thomas resides near Lake Arrowhead, California, with his wife, Charlotte.

Other Books by Thomas Settimi . . .

CONVERGENCE - Sky Scientific Press

Paperback (ISBN-13: 978-1419661518) 2nd Edition 2012

eBook Edition June 2012

www.ingramcontent.com/pod-product-compliance
Lightning Source LLC
LaVergne TN
LVHW091054080826
845145LV00002B/741